BRIDGE OVER STORMY WATER

A PWF SHORT WITH SNAP

MURKY MIDLIFE WATERS
BOOK TWO

JB LASSALLE

MIGHTY OAK
PUBLISHING SERVICES

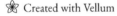

CHAPTER 1

I couldn't believe I was about to cross this damn bridge. Again.

Was it possible it had somehow become less sturdy in the past few weeks? Did bridges weather that quickly? There was absolutely nothing to back up that opinion other than my own paranoia. Even the deluge of storms we'd been having wouldn't make a bridge fall apart.

If anything, it had been a quiet month ... if you count discovering you're a mermaid and agreeing to fulfill a magical family legacy "quiet" that is.

Which, I kind of do. Particularly since my childhood best friend outed herself as a freaking goddess. And I'd spent the past two weeks talking to my pet alligator ... who talked back.

So yeah, my definition of normal had shifted.

Besides, mermaids shouldn't worry about bridges. If my car did plunge into the waters below, I should be able to swim out. Of course, the one and only time I'd seen my mermaid tail was when I was super drunk and had no control over it. And every effort I've made since to coax it back has failed and resulted in too many wine-induced headaches to count.

And maybe I'd spent the past two weeks in total denial that

I'm completely broke yet have to figure out how to renovate the supernatural building that is the only place I'd ever felt at home before we're all thrown out on our asses. And once I finished that, I'd have to figure out what the hell I was going to do next.

But if I couldn't be a freaking mermaid when I need to be, what use was it?!

I wasn't sure what was worse ... that I had to cross the bridge again, in the doggone rain, or that I was going back to New Orleans to see Pop. Begging my father for money at the tender young age of forty-seven wasn't exactly sitting well with me. Not that I believed for one second he wouldn't give it to me. Considering he'd known I was half-mermaid and never told me, I figured I had enough leverage to guilt him into helping if I needed it.

I gripped my stomach as it gurgled, then reached for another antacid. All this magic was giving me an ulcer.

I stopped glaring at the bridge long enough to stare at my phone when it alerted me via a pleasant chime I had no memory of setting that I had a text message.

Get over yourself and step on the gas.

I stuck my tongue out at the screen like a petulant child, then instantly looked around to make sure Iris couldn't see me. Odds were good she was back on her side of the island and knew I was being a coward, but it didn't hurt to double-check. Pissing off the Goddess of Rainbows, the ultimate of bridges, before crossing one seemed like a bad idea.

I ran my hand across the buttery leather of the steering wheel. It was a nicer car than the one I'd brought here, which Dimitri was still fixing. It was his fault the bridge was in such disrepair anyway, so it was the least he could do. I probably wouldn't hit a body on the other side like last time either. So, if I could just press my foot to the gas—

The phone dinged again. "I'm *going*."

The bridge creaked and groaned as I drove across. It was bitchier than I was. Despite the steady rain, the sun stayed high overhead, even as I reached the top arch and began the descent that would lead me to New Orleans.

I was relieved I'd made it across, but I couldn't help rubbing my stomach again as fresh dread settled in. One bridge down.

Another to go.

I put the north bridge to Treater's Way in my rearview mirror and headed to see Pop.

CHAPTER 2

"Still can't believe I voted for that asshole." Clementine, my Pop's neighbor, had greeted me that way since I'd stumbled to his doorway when Daniel kicked me out. She sat in her faded rocker on the shared porch of their shotgun duplex, her shock of tight, gray curls pulled into a long braid draped over the back. Beads were woven into the braid, and they tapped against the rocker as she moved.

"I'm sure he appreciated your vote, though. How's your back?"

"Damn good as long as I don't move it." Clementine chuckled and inhaled from the foul-smelling cigarette she'd lit. "He'll be glad to see you again, honey." Her wrinkled face lit into a generous expression of welcome that tilted her wide brown eyes upward.

"I'm glad to be here." Making it this far had given me a boost of confidence that held while I'd dipped through and around the many potholes on the unmarked, gravel street that led to my father's house. But now that I was staring at the faded yellow siding, hand hovered to knock on his tattered screen door, I was starting to doubt my life choices.

Pop opened the door before I could work up the nerve to

bang on it. "Hiya, Clem. Back okay?" With a wave to his neighbor, he beckoned me inside. I shuffled past him, waving at Clementine even as she picked up her phone to dial. News would be out that I was back in town soon enough, and I suddenly longed for the protective bubble of Bridge Island.

Pop's house opened into his living room, displaying his tattered leather couch with a TV tray propped nearby. An emerald green plate and silver fork rested on it, along with half a cup of coffee with so much cream it was almost white. The monotone drone of evening news emitted from the large screen TV I'd gifted him last Christmas. I rubbed at the small of my back, remembering how I'd held it up to the wall and hooked it onto the mount, while Daniel sat by and watched, mumbling that we should hire someone to do it.

"You got here faster than I expected." Pop put one big hand on the back of his neck, looking around as if the house wasn't always this messy.

"My friend's car is fast."

His fishing line and tackle box were heaped in the far corner, along with mud boots fresh with grime. I dipped my head toward it. ""Good day?"

"A few cats."

"Want me to fry them up for dinner?" A mental to-do list was taking shape in my mind, and the words were out before I realized it. Taking care of Pop was second-nature.

"Later, Misty. Wanna sit with me?"

"Coffee first?"

Pop sat on the couch, pushing the tray aside with a small groan as he lowered his massive frame. "Just made a fresh pot." He leaned back and turned up the volume, effectively drowning out any conversation. I stood there for a moment, running my finger through the dust on a nearby bookshelf. It was littered with glass jars, filled to the rim with seashells in various shapes and sizes. Broken, whole, chipped edges, or perfect. Pop didn't care. He grabbed them on the shores whenever he took his boat fishing, carried them in his tackle box, then brought them home to sit on his bookshelf. I cringed a little at the layer of grime on my finger.

I'd stayed here a few weeks after Daniel left me and had done a lot of cleaning to take my mind off things, but I'd never made it to this shelf. Now that I understood the contents, it tickled my heart a bit. Before, I'd thought they were just a fun collection rather than a way to hold onto the memory of my mother, who'd swam out to sea to live the mermaid life and left us behind. I wished I'd taken time to clean them for him, to make that connection more pleasant.

Since Pop sat down rather than get my coffee, I followed the narrow hallway to the kitchen on the left. There were no pictures on the wall, no remnants of my time living here as a young girl and until I moved into a dorm for college. No pictures of Mama either.

I returned with coffee for us both, mine almost black. He took his with a nod, eyes intent upon the chipper TV personality discussing traffic. I hovered near the shelf. I had no idea how to broach this topic, or how to tell him what I'd discovered. Usually, I would open my mouth and just let my brain unload. But this felt more delicate.

Mama had left us because she couldn't ignore the call of the sea to her mermaid heart. I'd never had a call until a few weeks ago, but if Pop knew it was beckoning me now, even if I was ignoring it, it would hurt. I picked up one of the mason jars of shells, my fingers sliding down the oily side.

"You know, Pop, some of these shells have sat in those jars so long they've got a nasty layer of grime. I was thinking we could turn them into picture frames, maybe get rid of some of the broken ones."

Pop shifted in his seat to face me. "Get rid of the broken ones? Why would we do that?"

"Oh, you know"—I blinked at his bewildered expression—"broken ones aren't super useful."

Pop shook his head. "Not everything has to serve a purpose, Misty Mae. Some of them are just for pretty."

I took one out and carried it to the kitchen, where I scrubbed both it and my hands clean. It was a nasty shade of yellow, with a jagged edge and a hole at the base. I peered closer, not even sure it was a shell. I took it back and held it in front of him.

"That's just a broken piece of glass, Pop."

Pop kept his eyes on the screen, so I returned to the shells and spent the remainder of the news, and the first half of Jeopardy, cleaning them. My stomach felt like it was on fire, but Pop ate every day at 7 without fail, so I finished cleaning and made us both dinner while he watched tv.

When Pat Sajak said goodnight, Pop joined me at the table. "How's Ruthie doing?"

"I think the same. I didn't really remember much until I got there." I shoveled catfish into my mouth, hoping he wouldn't understand me if my mouth was full. "She's gotten into a little bit of trouble, actually."

Pop's lip firmed. He knew that tactic. He dropped his fork and gestured at me. "Go on."

"She took a lien out on Bridge House to keep the cafe running."

"Cafe was your idea."

Well, that put my back up. "It was, way back when I was twelve and the B&B was open and I thought I'd live there forever. It's different now." I leaned forward. "It's the only thing that's keeping Bridge House going, Pop. And I don't want her to lose it. I convinced the bank to stay the loan for a few months, until the House was renovated and the rooms could be opened again."

A sadness I was used to shimmered in his eyes. "You aim to stay and help her?"

His voice wavered a touch, the unspoken hovered between us, and it soothed the feathers he'd inadvertently ruffled.

I reached across the table to take his hand. "A lot's changed since I went back there. It seems I've been living in a haze for thirty years." His eyes shifted away from mine with what might have been guilt. I squeezed his fingers until he looked back at me. "Now that the haze has lifted, I want to put to rights what fell apart when I left and didn't return." I waited a beat. "Part of what's happened there is my fault, Pop. I have to fix it."

He pulled his hand from the table to pat his stomach, rubbing it like he was Buddha, and it might give him wisdom. "You've always had a good heart, Misty, and always taken care of everyone. I suppose you can't help yourself." He patted my cheek, instantly making me feel like I was a little girl again. "What do you need from me?"

I sat up straight, drew in a deep breath, and blurted it out. "Money, Pop. I need lots of money for renovations."

The air between us went still, and his gaze wandered to the shelf of broken shells.

"Hey, Pop. I can get you more seashells." I waited until his eyes were on mine. "I can get anything you want from the water, and I promise to bring it back here to you."

It was the best way I knew to tell him I'd found my mermaid side without saying it outright. We needed to have that conversation, the real one, but I didn't have it in me. My focus had to be Bridge House.

I held his gaze firm, hoping he wouldn't see any doubt in my eyes. Doubt lingered in my heart, though. Since I'd discovered I was a mermaid, the siren song had only gotten stronger. But I had more ties to land than Mama did when she left. I had a daughter. And Aunt Ruth. And purpose.

Would I be able to go out into the water and ignore the siren song?

His lips worked beneath his bushy mustache. He sat back and jammed his finger on the remote to turn the volume up. "You have a plan, I take it?"

"I have the start of a plan."

Pop nodded, just a slight dip of his head, but I released my breath. "I'll get my checkbook after dinner."

CHAPTER 3

I wasn't sure what the record was for the number of belches in a fifteen-minute period, but I felt certain the enormous, dirty man sitting across from me at the cafe was topping it. He ran his grubby-nailed fingers across the plate to pick up the last of the crumbs from his sausage sandwich. I'd had to repress a snort when Kitty brought it to him, the casings so tight the meat wanted to bulge out. Not unlike the belly of the man who basically controlled my fate.

He licked the finger with a loud smack and grinned at me. "Yeah, Lucas told me a bit about the project. It's a big one. My men and I can handle it, though. We just need to draw up some blueprints of what you want."

"Actually, I have those ready for you." I slid a series of rolled up papers across the table. "I have a friend who's an architect. She drew up everything for us and we have supplies on order." I plastered a confident smile on my face. My architect friend was actually one of my future-ex-husband's staunch supporters, and though she'd often praised his strong stance on family values, she'd mysteriously disappeared from my life when word got out about what he did.

I'd called her anyway and admitted it had been hard, but that

11

this new project was just what I needed to feel like myself again. Within a few days I had everything I needed, and it had only cost me a little bit of my pride and another week at the center of the gossip circle.

Buford Higgins rolled them open and scanned the drawings. He may be more than a bit gross, but I recognized the knowledge in his eyes. He nodded, his mouth moving as he read through them and compared them to the lists of supplies and tasks I'd provided. I'd even created a timeline that, if god was willing and the creek didn't rise, would put us just in time and on budget. His hands caressed the blueprints as if they were the house itself, and a faint glimmer of excitement caused him to fidget in his seat. I waited, sipping an iced coffee. I hadn't slept in days as I'd pored through everything there was to know about remodeling and large construction projects, and I was beginning to feel more than a little punch drunk.

It was after noon, when the cafe started to dwindle to only the regulars. By now, I recognized most of them. An alleged dragon and his fiancée. The witch and her boyfriend. The man who looked disturbingly like Abraham Lincoln's ghost. That was Walter. Though I hadn't introduced myself yet, he seemed a friendly sort, patiently sitting in the corner as the day came and went. Kitty said he was a generous tipper.

I wondered where or how he got money since he always seemed to be sitting in that very spot. In fact, there was a shimmer about it I was just beginning to recognize as supernatural. Could I see them now, even with my tail playing hide and seek? I scanned the rest of the regulars, landing on Buford and squinting at him like he was a 3D painting. When he belched again, I chuckled to myself until Buford lifted his eyebrows at me. "Sorry. Lost in thought."

"Funny thoughts." He nodded his head, as if I wasn't really weird. "My wife does the same thing. Lots of internal dialogue." The comment was astute enough to shut me up. "These look real good, Ms. Misty. I can get a crew here first thing tomorrow morning."

A little spark of a thrill rushed through me. "That would be perfect, thank you!"

"Yes ma'am." He extended his hand, and I shook it then wiped my fingers on my lap. "So, I'll send you the contract tonight—it'll be an email from my wife, Peggy—just be sure it's signed and the deposit is ready in the morning. With you ordering supplies it should go fast."

It had to. "And you'll be extra careful not to disturb the kitchen and cafe area along this side, right? It's our only revenue stream at the moment."

"Yes ma'am." He rose, his stomach pushing the tiny table between us which made a loud scooting sound. I got up and followed him toward the stairs. "We'll start by setting up the construction barricades here and here." I followed his hands as he pointed to spots along the porch. "Some basic demo that we'll have to do early, that part will get loud but we gotta do it before it gets too hot. We'll set up temporary steps up the front door if you need 'em, but I recommend just using the side door through the cafe while we fix up the porch."

"The porch." My heart sank just a little. "Oh, I see, you plan to start outside."

"Yes ma'am. The lumber will come in first, and getting this safe should be the priority."

He was right. The stairs were sketchy, and I was tired of picking splinters out of my finger every night after we sat out. But ...

"I wonder if there's any way we can start with one of the upstairs bedrooms." He cocked an eyebrow at me. "That one." I opened the front door and pointed toward the rickety banister that towered above us on the third floor. "I know it doesn't make sense to start with one bedroom all the way up there, but if we could repair the balcony and put the room back to rights, well ..."

It didn't make sense. Not in a way I could explain to a near stranger, or even myself. He scratched his thick, black beard and surveyed the space above us, shielding his eyes with his hands. "That balcony has quite a view. Is it your room?"

My heart let out a dull thud. "It was my parent's room when we lived here. I always wanted it."

I wanted it still. It was wrong, and it made no sense, but sleeping downstairs made me feel like a guest. And I didn't want to feel like a guest. Not for one summer or even one more week. "It won't take much, you can see on the plans. The floors need sanding and refurbishing. The walls need fresh paint. I think the balcony took a hit during one of the hurricanes, not sure which."

"Katrina." His voice came out soft, a wistful reminder of a horrible time. I understood the tone. No matter how resilient we claimed to be, each of us had a hurricane story that shook us to the core. "I surveyed the land out here for your aunt a few months after. She said most of the balconies took a beating."

Both of us shook our heads, a common New Orleanian trait when we went back in our memories to the months after Katrina. I liked Buford. He was brash and loud and gassy, but he had a good heart and a shrewd eye. Even if he'd come from Lucas's recommendation, that gave me hope that I wasn't dealing with a crook.

And I had to like him ç he was the only one available. Not a single other contractor was willing to take the job, and I had a sneaking suspicion Lucas wanted it that way, though I didn't understand why. Still, Buford was from Treater's Way and had worked on some of the construction for Illusion Square, so I felt a bit better about him.

And I was desperate for this to work. Even if I hadn't slept in a week while planning out the details and ordering the materials so he could start as soon as possible. There was just one thing I wanted.

"So that room, if we could, will be where we start." Then maybe, just maybe, I could call Bridge House a home again.

At least for now.

14

CHAPTER 4

*B*uford waved goodbye and peeled out of the tiny parking area. A spray of dust and rocks followed his truck, and the sound of his engine faded, but didn't rev down like it should have if he'd slowed to cross the bridge. Which meant he took it at full speed.

I wondered what deity I could pray to that might keep the bridge intact long enough for us to renovate. We'd need materials and big machines and I had zero faith it would hold up to that kind of scrutiny. I turned back toward the cafe just as a flash of blond hair disappeared around the corner. The hairs on my arms lifted. What was Lucas Carpenter doing at the cafe?

Bile burned the back of my throat. I didn't trust him, and his fake charm oozed over me like slime every time we met. I had half a mind to ask him to leave, even if I didn't have a reason to. But a mystical lullaby circled itself around me, and my body angled itself toward the shore before I realized I'd moved. I was still for a moment, pulled in two directions as my duty to Bridge House and my siren song both beckoned me.

Then a different kind music stifled the song in my head, and I smiled at the familiar tune. Dimitri Carpenter's boots jutted out from underneath my Jeep not far from where I stood, and an old, digital radio was balanced on the hood of my mom's convertible blasting the tinny twang of a guitar. I paused there, cringing as my inner siren protested.

One of his boots tapped in time to the music, and a glint of sunlight caught the tip of the bumper, giving it an iridescent glow. A memory popped into my head, of Dimitri telling me he'd pulled the Jeep over here when it stalled at North Bridge, and my heart did a little jig as a puzzle piece clicked into place.

"Hey, Dimitri, are you a real troll?"

From underneath the car there was a distinct *bonk* followed by a violent curse. He slid out and fixed me with his signature glare, a deep red welt already emerging on his forehead. "What did you just ask me?"

"Uhm ... sorry about that." I shoved my hands in the pockets of my shorts to keep them from touching the bruise. "It just struck me that if Iris is an actual goddess and I'm a mermaid that, well, you might actually *be* a troll."

He stretched his arm overhead to reach for a cloth, revealing a hint of his thin waist. I took a step back, as if his hotness would grab onto me like a cartoon sliver of smoke and make me straddle him.

He blinked at me now, the round gold of his eyes boring into mine. "Want to catch me up?"

With a self-conscious laugh, I looked down at the ground, kicking gravel, cursing my inability to keep thoughts inside my brain where they belonged. "You live under a bridge. You're grumpy as hell. And Iris calls you troll." I shrugged and tapped one finger to my head. "I made the connection."

My heart pounded in my throat. He had a way of staring at me that was so intense I felt naked. I wasn't a fan. Not that I didn't look great naked. Thanks to Daniel's cure-cancer-through-diet-and-exercise obsession, I was a pretty damn healthy forty-seven-year-old. But dating was not on my radar. Plus, there was the whole "I hated his brother" thing. Then again, I think he did, too.

As if I'd conjured him with my thoughts, Lucas strolled past us on his way to South Bridge.

"Dimitri. Misty." He lifted a to-go cup in a wave, smiling as if he hadn't a care in the world. I hoped Kitty spit in his coffee.

"Gosh, it just hit me." I flipped my eyes away from Lucas and back to Dimitri. "Is your half-brother a troll? Now *that* I can believe."

"Misty." Dimitri's voice was soft and laced with compassion. "When did you learn you were a mermaid?"

"A few weeks ago, I drank too much wine, had a conversation with Norbert—by the way, did you know he talks?—then went to bed and passed out. When I woke up ..." I waved my hand like it swam through water.

He crossed his arms, leaning against my Jeep as he took me in fixing me with a look that made my toes curl. "Stop staring at me like I have gills."

To my surprise, he laughed. "Do you?"

I rolled my eyes. "I did have webbed hands, though. It was trippy. Now tell me." I dropped my voice. "Are you a troll?"

I held my breath while he hesitated to answer. Maybe he was debating trusting me, or maybe he was considering calling a hospital. Honestly, at this point it could go either way. The more people corroborated the truth about the supernatural, the more I felt like I'd dived completely into my own illusion.

Then he nodded, and I exhaled. "Wow. And Lucas?"

"Yes, but not the same kind." Dimitri glared in the direction of the bridge his brother had just crossed. "We have different fathers. But our mother was human."

There it was again. The deep sadness in his voice when he mentioned his mother. "I get it. Mine didn't die but apparently she swam away from me." An instant of kinship passed between us. "So, if you're a troll and your brother is a troll, why is the North Bridge so crappy?"

That connection vanished. I took a step back from the rage he suddenly radiated, as if it might reach out and attack me. "Sorry, I didn't mean it to come out so rude." Crap. I would think about that one for days.

He dragged fingers through his hair, staining them with grease. "It's not you. It's complicated."

I chewed on the inside of my mouth. "I understand complicated."

He took a deep swig from a bottle of water, keeping his eyes on me like I might launch a sneak attack. When he wiped his mouth with his sleeve, I considered it. "I heard you were trying to help Ruth. Lucas mentioned he extended the loan."

I raised one eyebrow. "That seems like a business matter that Lucas should not be sharing."

"Except you are part of Treater's Way now, and everyone knows everything."

I sighed. He had a point. "Yes, I'm helping Ruth. And as long as we are sharing business, I don't mind telling you that I think your brother was an ass to put her in this position in the first place."

He snorted again, and one side of his mouth lifted. "I'm not a big fan of Lucas."

"You're enough of a fan that he told you my business."

Dimitri lifted his lip as he glanced over my shoulder. Without following his stare, I figured Iris was approaching. She tended to find me when she had a free period, so we could hang at the shoreline with Norbert.

I braced myself for their sniping and snapped my fingers in front of him. "I appreciate you fixing the car, I truly do, but you don't have to waste your lunch hour here."

"What's up, troll?" Iris's voice dripped disdain, and while I was happy to see my best friend, I wasn't in the mood for their back and forth. I put my hands between them, pretending not to notice the subtle flex of Dimitri's muscles under my palm.

"Please don't start, you two. I've had a day and a half already and it's only one."

Dimitri turned from Iris, the unexpected concern in his eye

catching me off guard. "Did something happen with the contractor?"

"Buford? I mean, aside from him belching he seems ... solid." A creeping worry snuck up my spine. "Is there something about Buford I should know?"

Dimitri snorted. "You should know not to trust Lucas, and he came from Lucas."

"He's the only one who is available." I didn't like how defensive I sounded, even to my own ears. "You know what guys, I appreciate your feedback and all but this is my problem now."

"Whatever." Dimitri finished his water, then lowered himself to the rolling platform. "I just want to be done with all of this."

He continued to mumble, even as his torso disappeared under the Jeep. When I tore my gaze away from him, Iris was watching me with a curious expression.

"What?" I snapped.

The corner of her painted lips lifted into a grin. "Nothing. I just came to say hi."

I stalked toward the shores to see Norbert, not bothering to see if Iris was coming. She caught up to me. "Don't make me run in designer sandals, please."

"Sorry." I slowed my pace, looping our arms. "I'm snippy today."

"Why?"

I waved an anxious hello to Norbert, but my eyes caught the lap of water, the gentle rise and fall of it, and a longing deep within me rose. "I don't know."

But even as the lie left my lips, the siren song beckoned.

CHAPTER 5

*T*he banging assembly of a construction crew jolted me awake the next morning. I wasn't a fan of 5 a.m. I was of the firm opinion that anything active before seven was suspicious. And for two weeks everyone in Bridge House had been up by five when Buford and his crew arrived, slinging hammers and jokes with the same speed, acting as if they'd been awake for hours and pretty much pissing me off just for existing.

It wasn't their fault. The nighttime jaunts to the shore with too much wine in the hopes of bringing my tail forward were starting to wreak havoc. My song was deafening in my head. Combined with the all-day banging and drilling, my head ached so badly even the roots of my hair hurt.

We were one month down and nothing was going as planned. Every day, some new problem emerged. From faulty wiring on lights that had worked the day before to mold in places where no water could have existed. And my protests about starting with the porch had been rendered moot by nonstop rain. Our schedule was out the window, and I was winging it each day.

I really needed coffee. And water. But ever since construction started, Lucas had taken to dropping by for breakfast or just before closing. Just to see how things were progressing he'd tell me, but his mere presence set me on edge. Meanwhile, Aunt Ruth trotted off to Illusion Square each morning, leaving me alone with the house and the cafe and the noise.

I'd asked for this.

Even as my throat burned, my stomach growled. I was abnormally hungry. And I had a craving I couldn't quite place.

It had to be greasy. Hangover food. And coffee that was super strong. Maybe darker than I usually took it. Chicory. I wanted chicory.

But the food ... I couldn't figure out what it was, I just knew it would make me feel better.

When I entered the kitchen, the head chef Sam and our waitress Kitty were engaged in a heated bicker. Sam hovered over her a good two feet, his beard even scruffier than normal. Kitty rolled her eyes as he pointed his finger in her direction. She smiled at me when I walked in then took two fingers to her forehead in a mock salute in my direction.

"Hey," I said. "What's the argument today?"

Sam kept his eyes on Kitty, but raised his voice to speak to me. "Kitty thinks we need to add a new item to the menu." He shook his head as if I might commiserate despite walking into the conversation two minutes earlier.

Kitty leaned against the counter with her arms crossed. "I'm just telling him what the customers are saying." She smacked her gum, blew a big bubble, then popped it in Sam's direction. She had the beginnings of a third ponytail, the same flaming orange as the other two, but shorter and stubbier like new hair growth. "They want a new menu item. I've had three customers ask for it in the past week. Shouldn't we listen to demand?"

I propped myself on the bar stool where a hot mug of coffee waited for me. Bless that Kitty. I pulled the mug to my lips and closed my eyes with a happy sigh at the first sip. Whatever had happened last night, and whatever I'd woken up to this morning, it was already feeling like a distant memory. A bad dream brought on by too much wine. Okay, maybe there was some weird reminder in my head, a memory really far away that I couldn't quite latch onto. Something about a breakfast item that I used to eat ...

"... Menu item?" Kitty's expression transformed into a mischievous grin. She looked me dead in the eye.

I blinked her back into focus. "Huh?"

Her grin disappeared, and the sardonic teen expression I was more used to bored into me. "I said, don't you think taquitos would be an awesome new menu item?"

Taquitos! *That* was what I was craving. I remembered now from my college days of too much drinking how much I loved them, and how they soothed a hungover tummy. I licked my lips. "Absolutely. Yum."

Sam lifted his arms in exasperation, but a thin smile was hiding under his beard. "You two and your big ideas for this menu. I've managed this menu for thirty-five years without input from any of ya."

"And you've done it perfectly, my Sam." I took another sip of coffee and winked at him. "I used to eat taquitos all the time in college. They're the perfect hangover food. And if we repair North Bridge and get the New Orleans tourists back that would be quite a boon." I perked up as the idea wormed through me. "We can offer a service! We'll drive guests into the city, let them get good and drunk, then bring them home safe and sound. We'll leave two aspirin and a glass of water on their nightstand, make sure they are tucked in safely. And the next morning"—I smacked my lips—"hangover food for breakfast! What's the Cajun equivalent of a taquito?"

Sam shook his head at me. "You don't even have one bedroom finished yet, and you are already planning a service where we get people drunk and feed them food I've never heard of?"

"You've never heard of a taquito?" I clasped my hands to my chest in mock horror. "It's, like, totally sort of a breakfast burrito but way better." I dipped my head and raised my voice, putting on my best sorority girl accent. Beside Sam, Kitty snickered.

"That's redundant. We have breakfast tacos on the menu. You had one your first damn day back." Sam turned away, muttering to himself as if the conversation was over. Kitty slid over to refill the coffee mug I didn't realize I drained, nudging my favorite creamer across the island to me.

I nodded my head and chuckled. This place was weird, and I was beginning to like it. I gripped my mug with two hands, watching as Sam alternated between three pans of food and Kitty loaded plates into the dishwasher. They fought a lot, but they were a team at the end of it.

Every now and again, Sam cast a glance toward Kitty that I pretended not to notice. The irritation in his eyes would disappear, and his stare would linger on her shoulders with a longing that tore at my heart.

I searched my memories to my first meeting with Sam. He'd arrived here the day I sent out word about needing a chef, and because I was twelve I never stopped to find that strange. He'd taught me how to make a roux, describing the process as if he were describing a beautiful woman. When my sassy twelve-year-old self had mentioned that, he'd called me a Cajun word I didn't understand and probably didn't want to. But underneath that gruff goat exterior of his, there'd always been tenderness. Whether it made sense to me or not, Sam belonged to Bridge House.

It occurred to me as I watched them that I wasn't sure who on the island, or in Treater's Way, was a supernatural. I'd already seen a strange fox scampering around the woods that looked suspiciously like Kitty. Her name still didn't sit right—everything about her was foxlike. Her movements were sharp and swift, her clothes flame red to match her hair. I wanted to find out more, but asking about their supernatural identity felt rude. But if I wanted to understand the purpose of Bridge House better, then two of the island's staples seemed like a great place to start.

"Hey, have either of you guys ever ... talked to Norbert?"

A look I couldn't decipher passed between Sam and Kitty. She lifted her eyebrow at him and cocked her head to the side. Her eyes narrowed over her shrewd face. Sam shook his head. "No way. You're the messenger."

You're the messenger. I didn't know what it meant, but that subtle acknowledgement brought a tingling in my toes and my legs, and the stirring of something deep within me. Like calling like. Every time I got a little comfortable here, or pulled up a memory from the past, something inside me woke up.

My stomach tumbled enough to make me regret my morning longing for chicory, but I decided to embrace it. The way through was forward. "What does that mean, 'you're the messenger'?"

Kitty and Sam continued to stare at one another. Then she sighed and looked at me. She leaned her forearms on the island so she could meet my eyes, and her midriff shirt rose just a little higher exposing more of her skin. Behind her, Sam's eyes widened, and he swallowed.

"Misty, sometimes things are more than they seem. And sometimes, if you look closer, and tap into your memories, you'll see what's been there all along."

She straightened up, grabbing her order pad from the side counter. "We've all talked to Norbert." With a final look at Sam that was uncomfortably knowing, she slid out the glass doorway.

I kept my eyes on her as she greeted customers and scribbled on her notepad. Sam had resumed his perch at the stove, humming in his usual way under his breath like he was singing to his food. But there was something different in the hum. It was quieter than normal, as if he was waiting for me to ask a question.

Nerves bundled inside me. The tingling intensified. And in a flash, I saw myself in my twelve-year-old body, swinging my legs from this very bar stool, while Sam hummed over a grilled cheese sandwich he was making me. It was more like nostalgia than a memory, as what came to mind wasn't what happened but how I'd felt. Like I was in a safe place with my very large, brash and grumpy uncle. Like he'd been part of my family. My heart swelled with love for Sam, then and now, as a tenuous thread from the past connected to the present.

He wanted to say more. I couldn't explain how I knew it, but I understood that the tone of his hum and the way he wasn't saying anything at all was a sign that he would answer my questions outright, if only I asked them. And the thought of that flooded me with fear, so I switched tactics. "You know she's too young for you, right?"

Sam flipped a pancake then turned to me. "What are you yapping about over there?"

"Kitty. She's really cute, and I'm pretty sure she's older than she looks. But don't you think it's a little too close to robbing the cradle?"

Sam held my gaze for an uncomfortably long time before putting his back to me and facing the stove. I heaved myself off the bar stool, grabbed the coffee, and prepared to head upstairs. I stopped in the doorway and turned him. "Breakfast burritos are really good. if you made one right now, I would totally eat it. And I'm sure you would make it perfectly. We wouldn't have to call them taquitos."

I turned from the door at his sweet big uncle smile. "Misty." When I returned to the doorway, he winked at me again. "Kitty is twice my age."

CHAPTER 6

*O*nce I had the construction crew started upstairs, I wandered back into the cafe. The words Kitty had said earlier were still nagging at me: that things here weren't always what they seem. I still wasn't entirely clear what the purpose of Bridge House was, or what I was supposed to do other than welcome people to it. Maybe it was naive of me to assume we'd fix the house and keep it running, but I wanted something to cling to. And once I solved this problem, I still had plenty of other ones to tackle.

Like how the heck does a mermaid find her tail? And what the heck does the hostess of Bridge House even do?

I leaned against the railing and surveyed the customers in the cafe, scowling as Lucas dipped his head in greeting while lifting a forkful of lettuce. Aside from him, only a few of the twelve tables were occupied. One of them was the man who looked like Abraham Lincoln and he caught my eye as I stared in his direction. He'd sat in the same corner table every day. I'd once asked Ruth about him, she had just smiled in her usual absent-minded Ruth way and told me that he would go when he was ready.

He gave me a long, slow smile and nodded his head, which I took as an invitation to walk over.

"Do you mind if I join you?" Before he could answer, I pulled out the opposite chair and sat down. Like magic, Kitty put a plate and a tall glass of water in front of me. The plate contained scrambled eggs, bacon, hashed potatoes, and cheese wrapped in a thick flour tortilla. Sour cream, tomatoes, lettuce and a salsa I wouldn't touch sat as garnish next to it.

A breakfast burrito. I nearly whimpered.

Forgetting my manners for a moment, I bit into the luxurious item, closed my eyes, and moaned at the heavenly taste. It was like all the dehydration and foggy headedness from the night before was wiped away as I chewed and swallowed. "Bless you, Sam."

"Indeed, he's quite a gift in the kitchen." I jolted my eyes open, realizing I'd forgotten not-Lincoln was there. He steepled his fingers and smiled, his face serene and amused.

"Sorry, I forgot you were there for a minute, what with this amazing breakfast in front of me. I'm Misty, Ruth's niece. I don't think we've met before and I thought today seemed like a good time to come over and introduce myself."

"Today seems like a good day to do anything. Call me Walter."

Up close, his resemblance to the late president was even more uncanny. It wasn't just that the hair was natural and the beard was his. It was something about the way his face crinkled when he smiled, the careful and deliberate way he moved. There was a knowledge and wisdom in his eyes, a timbre in his voice.

I could almost believe it was actually Lincoln. Except for the tattoo of a penny peeking out from the edge of his sleeve.

"So, what's your story, Walter?"

He chuckled softly and leaned back in his chair. As I chewed, my body relaxed, and it struck me that I could see Walter's chair. Through Walter. I shook my head to clear the image, and he was no longer translucent.

"Oh, I don't know. My story has been told before, I suppose. There's many a movie and book about me."

Granted, I was basing my image of Abraham Lincoln off of *Bill and Ted's Excellent Adventure*, but hearing him speak was uncanny. I debated what to say in response, how to avoid sounding awkward, and drew a blank. "So, are you an Abraham Lincoln impersonator?"

His smile widened. "Indeed, I am. I do some of his speeches in the city." His brow furrowed as he turned his gaze in the direction of North Bridge. "Now that you mention it, I think I just finished a show."

"What do you mean?"

He pressed his lips together and strained his eyes down the road. "A local playwright contacted me about a show he was writing for Le Petit." He shook his head and chuckled. "It was most unusual."

"Do you mean the theater in the French Quarter?" At his nod, I bit down on my smile. The theater showcased everything from thought-provoking drama to burlesque drag shows, and I couldn't help but wonder which end of the spectrum he'd found himself on.

"Somehow, the after party led to a discussion of Bridge House and rumors of a very large alligator. So, a few of us found a ride from an unscrupulous cab driver who assured us passage but had the nerve to stop as we reached North Bridge."

"A cab driver, huh?" It was a strange choice of words these days, to mention a taxi as opposed to ride share. Warning bells sounded in my mind as I realized he sat here all day without a phone.

"Yes, naturally. Although I assured him I would tip more than a *me* dollar bill." He paused to let me chuckle at his pun. "He said the bridge was most unstable, and that a troll would forbid his passing. Rapscallion." He huffed out a breath at the memory, even as a strange chill passed through me. He brushed nonexistent lint from his lapel. "Nonetheless, my friends and I carried on, eager to pursue our destiny." As he leaned forward, he dropped his voice. "And though I claim to be a teetotaler, I confess to being more than a little inebriated."

"Been there," I mumbled. "So, you and your drunk friends decided to walk eight miles across a rickety old bridge in the middle of the night?"

He tapped one long finger to his nose. "As I said, too much bourbon." He smiled at the memory. "We paused midway across the bridge to admire the view and decided on a spontaneous scene from our well-reviewed play. I was quite taken with the buxom Mary Todd, so I gave it my all." His brow furrowed again, as if the happy memory had been immediately replaced with a different one. He held his hands in front of him, then flipped his palms backwards and forwards. He removed his stovepipe hat, turning it in front of him as if it were a foreign object. He scratched his head, staring at the hat in wonder.

I cleared my throat, waiting on him to continue. When he didn't, I touched my hand to his lightly. "Everything okay, Walter?"

Walter looked up at me like he didn't know I was there, his body wavering like a silhouette. "Pardon me for asking such a strange question, but are my clothes wet?"

"They don't seem to be. Wait." They hadn't been wet, not when I sat down or any time before. But water trickled down the side of his face, and damp patches appeared on his suit. I leaned to the side and looked down at the ground to see if there was a puddle beneath him. There was a water stain, as if water had once upon a time gathered there, but no actual puddle. I sat up again and gave him my most reassuring smile. "You look dry as a bone, Walt."

Walter shook his head, muttering to himself. "I really should meet up with my group. I'm running very late."

As he rose, the chair remained where it was. He trotted down the stairs, breaking into a slow jog down the road to North Bridge. Although the burrito had done its job, and I was feeling better physically, the encounter with Walter, compiled with everything else, left me shaken and unsteady.

I took my plate to the kitchen and loaded it into the dishwasher. The walls seemed to swell around me, as if they too were treading water.

"What?" I said to the cabinet. "What am I supposed to do?" The cabinet shuddered, opening and closing as if heaving a disappointed sigh. I glared at it. "I don't understand you," I told the house. "Not one bit."

"Misty, might I have a moment?"

Lucas's overly proper voice soured my mood even further. It wasn't just how polite he sounded, as if we were crossing paths at a formal tea. He'd caught me talking to the damn kitchen. I braced myself before fixing a false smile on my face. "Of course, Lucas. How can I help you?"

"Well, I'm concerned about our progress."

My fake smile widened. "*Our* progress is going just fine, Lucas. We've had a few minor setbacks, but nothing I can't handle." The ceiling creaked like it disagreed with me. I lifted my eyes to find the drywall above us warping. The sensation of a balloon about to burst filled my chest. "Excuse me, Lucas, but I think I'm needed upstairs."

As I stepped toward the center of the kitchen, Lucas grabbed my forearm and yanked me backwards, his manicured fingernails digging deep into my arm.

"What the hell?" I was shouting, but if he heard me he gave no indication. The ceiling moaned. Specks of dust rained down, covering the island. And a pain that was both mine and foreign dropped into my stomach, as if I were flying downhill too fast.

Then the ceiling broke open, the house shook, and my mother's bed, the very bed I'd coveted from a young age and hoped to claim as my own one day, landed with a deafening thud on the kitchen floor.

CHAPTER 7

*I*t hit the island in the center first, shattering a stack of plates and saucers awaiting their turn in the dishwasher. Kitty pushed her way through the patio doors, where the last remaining customers pressed hands and noses to the glass. She edged around the bed, now precariously positioned with the foot on the floor and the head half-on and half-off the island, to reach Sam and place a soothing hand on his massive bicep.

On one of Sam's first days in the cafe, he'd cut his finger. It was a deep enough cut that blood soaked through all of the towels I'd wrapped around his hand. With the haze of the bridge removed, that memory came flooding back to me. I'd sobbed openly, pushing him out the door while he chuckled at my panic.

"It's a few stitches, little one, nothing to fuss over," he'd told me, as if I were the one who needed comforting. Meanwhile, his normally ruddy cheeks were growing pale from blood loss.

Sam was tough. There were few tougher.

But the giant four-poster bed in the middle of his sanctuary was more than even he could manage. He let out a garbled noise, a cross between a moan and a scream. Giant tears fell from his eyes and soaked his beard. Kitty turned off the burners of the stove and whispered in his ear, though I'm not sure he heard a word she uttered.

The front door slammed and heavy footsteps padded down the stairs. Dimitri and Buford reached the entrance to the kitchen simultaneously, their broad shoulders pushing through the doorway in their rush to see the damage. If I weren't in so much pain, I might have found it comical. But Bridge House mourned, and as surely as I stood there, I felt the ache in my bones.

My connection to the house was growing. It struck me that some of the frustration and anxiety I'd experienced over the past few weeks came from the house itself. While I'd assumed it was being petulant because it didn't like the colors I'd chosen or the instructions I'd provided, I began to wonder if the house was fighting another force. I tilted my head toward Lucas, catching the unmistakably smug satisfaction in his eyes before he could plaster his mask back on. My stomach rolled in disgust, confirming my suspicions.

"Damnedest thing." Buford approached the bed, staggering backwards when it tilted and creaked as if it might attack him. He lifted sheepish eyes to meet mine. "We've been sanding the floors up there. I guess it was too heavy without the additional reinforcement?"

I'd heard the expression seeing red before, but I'd never actually experienced it until now. Between the barely contained smile on Lucas's face, the complete confusion of Buford's slack jaw, and Sam's unchecked anguish, a haze of red tunneled my vision and clouded the edges of my sight.

"Are you—" I inhaled deeply, taking a steadying breath. "Are you asking me if that is what happened?" I was doing my best not to explode, not to let the layer of anger seething in my core come to the surface and rage. Buford looked as befuddled as I felt, which at least told me that he hadn't done this on purpose.

Or so I hoped.

"Well"—Lucas stepped forward, rubbing his hands together as

if he had an evil plan—"this is most unfortunate. However, we can be grateful that no one was hurt. Right, Sam? Kitty?"

An expression I had never seen crossed Sam's face. One of pure rage so aggressive I thought Lucas might wither beneath it. He had, at least, the good sense to back himself to the wall. Sam growled out his answer.

"No one was hurt. But they sure could have been." His voice was tight, as if he too were trying to control what was boiling inside.

For a moment, no one spoke. Dimitri watched me from the corner of the kitchen, one eyebrow lifted. I scanned the sea of faces and realized they were all waiting for me to respond. To act.

Because, like it or not, Bridge House was my responsibility right now.

"Kitty, would you be kind enough to step outside and tell everyone that the cafe is closed until further notice?" My voice cracked, and my heart broke into pieces at Sam's devastated expression when he looked at mine. "Sam, take the rest of the day off."

He removed his apron, and my throat clogged as I realized I'd never seen him without it. Then he came to me and wrapped his beefy arms around my shoulders. I leaned into him, afraid for one moment that I would break, then pushed him away and patted his cheek with what I hoped was a sweet smile. It felt more like a grimace.

"Everyone, please leave. Lucas, I believe you overstayed your welcome."

If he was surprised by my directness, it didn't show. He removed his phone from his pocket, looking at the screen as if he'd suddenly received an important message and had been called away, and stepped out with a brisk nod. Dimitri took one step closer to me, but I held my hands up to him. "I'm asking *everyone* to leave. Buford, send your crew home for the day as well."

After everyone shuffled out, I leaned against the counter and stared at the bed, hoping it might disappear. Bits of dust and insulation drifted down from the ceiling, where wood planks dangled from the massive hole the bed created on its way to the kitchen.

Funny. I'd always thought the balcony would fall first.

"This is your way of telling me not to work on the bedroom, isn't it?" I no longer felt silly talking to the house, as I could feel the house's emotions as surely as I felt my own. It wasn't happy with this development. And I didn't think it had shoved the bed through the ceiling.

I didn't understand the house's purpose any more than I understood my own, but I knew that much.

I wasn't sure what to do about the bed, not yet, but I could clean around it. I set about washing dishes and scrubbing counters, pretending not to notice that fresh plaster replaced what I wiped off. Before long, the area surrounding the bed looked untouched.

I wandered upstairs to peek into the bedroom and see the mess from eye-level. The wallpapers, still faded with those ugly roses, stared back at me. I shook my head, and laughter bubbled to the surface. I wasn't happy; this was not the laughter of mirth. This was delirium. As sure as I was standing there, I was about to hit my limit, and I had no idea what to do.

Then, a whisper stirred within. It was somewhat familiar, the sensation of something inside me waking up, and as it stretched and yawned, a soft, sweet sound came to me. It was the voice of a female, humming and joyful, and her tune was as melodic as ocean waves. At first, I turned to make sure it wasn't Aunt Ruth. I didn't want her to see the damage until I could explain it to her.

But that wasn't a song she'd ever hummed, and that wasn't her voice. It was mine. It was my siren song, louder and more clear than ever before.

I closed my eyes to tune into the sound of myself, humming and joyful, and free. A sensation I never felt before washed over me. I lifted my head toward the balcony, a breeze cooling my face.

The sea called.

The water, beckoned my inner mermaid, enticing me to come out and play.

That was a hell of a lot easier than dealing with this mess.

It was time to find out what happened if I answered it.

CHAPTER 8

J followed my song to the water, sliding down the levee
at twice my normal speed, stopping only when my toes
hit the edge. It was colder than I thought it would be, brisk
against my feet, and the shock of it halted the song. But only for a
moment.

Bridge House was empty. I had no way to make money for it.
There was no way I would finish on time now that I also had to
fix a kitchen and a ceiling. Lucas's bank would foreclose, and we
would lose our family home. The home that had been in my
family for generations. The home where I'd grown up and that I'd
forgotten about somehow.

The home where I'd discovered that magic was real.

My Aunt's home.

Sam and Kitty's home.

All of that was behind me. But before me was water. Murky
and brown, not at all appealing to consider swimming in. But the
very idea of a swim made the song sing louder. It filled my ears, a
rush as if I held a seashell to the side of my face. It roared through
me, demanding my soul answer it. I'd never experienced anything
so strong and sure in my life.

But, I had no idea what to do.

The water rippled, and I glanced to my left, unsurprised to find Norbert floating there.

"Hey." I waved my hand at him, his eyes barely visible above the surface, the hint of his body forming moss green shapes against the brown. "Can you teach me how to be a mermaid?"

He didn't answer right away, just watched me. I plopped to my butt and brought my knees to my chest, wrapping my arms tight around them. "Everything fell apart in there. My mom's bed is in the kitchen now, and we had to close the cafe. Even Walter disappeared, and who knows where he went." A tear slid down my cheek. "I'm pretty much failing at being human, no matter what side of the bridge I'm on. I'm done asking my tail to emerge. I'm just going to force it out."

He glided closer, edging his long snout so that it rested alongside me. The bumps of his skin pressed into my side, and though it wasn't sweet and cuddly like petting a cat, I felt the same comfort. I placed one of my hands on his back. "Thank you."

"It's not that hard to do." His words made his entire body move. I would never get used to that. "You just have to let go. Your instinct is to be a mermaid, just as much as it is to be human. You have to trust it."

I snorted. Trusting my instincts was not a specialty of mine. Second guessing myself and carrying on inner dialogue that exhausted me and exasperated others. That was my specialty.

"Do you hear it?"

I knew he meant the call of the sea. I nodded. "Do you?"

"Not like you, but your mother explained it to me once."

That got me. This was what she'd heard. This was the call that she'd had to endure until she couldn't any longer. Did Ruth hear it still? I'd have to ask her about it.

If I returned.

"I get it now."

Norbert growled. I think it was a growl, it's very hard to say. But maybe he was acknowledging my words. I closed my eyes and let the song wash over me. There was a tingling in my feet and calves. Was that my tail emerging? I popped one eye open. Just feet. Just legs. I sighed. "This is going to be harder than I thought."

Norbert shifted backwards, sinking his body into the water until only his head was on the shore. "Why don't you put your toes back in? Maybe get a little wet and see if that helps."

I scooted a bit closer, wincing as the shells and rocks underneath me scratched my skin. I'd had my toes in before, and I'd always been an overachiever, so I let both feet rest in the water. A few minnows scattered as I disturbed the sand bed. They returned a moment later to nibble on my nail polish. "At least I'm getting a pedicure."

I tapped both feet to the tune of the song. Waiting.

Norbert watched me.

The tingle grew stronger and spread to my thighs. It was like both legs had fallen asleep and were just waking up. Not quite painful, but it didn't feel good. The tingle spread, though, lifting through my core and into my chest. It felt invasive and strange, so I shoved it down.

"Don't fight it," Norbert snapped.

"Easy for you to say," I snapped back.

"Maybe you should try taking your clothes off." I lifted my eyebrows at him and he grinned. "Your mom never wore clothes. At least not pants. She'd wear a dress and as soon as she hit the water, she'd leave it on the shore until she returned."

The mental image of that flashed in me. My mom's bright, flowy dresses that barely reached midway down her thigh. Always in lovely colors and soft materials. I remembered sneaking into her bedroom right before Pop took us to New Orleans. She was gone, but all of her clothes were still in the wardrobe, and I'd thought that was so strange. I'd climbed in and closed the door, almost too big to fit, and buried myself in the scent of her and the softness of that material. "I took one of them with me."

"What's that?"

"Nothing." I shook my head at Norbert. "Just another memory coming back to me."

Before I could talk myself out of it, I jumped to my feet. Norbert twitched in the water. "What's wrong?"

He made that growling noise again. "You scared me."

I couldn't help but laugh. "You know you could eat me, right?"

With a flick of his tail, Norbert turned around. "I'm ignoring that. Now take your clothes off."

"Okay, sure." I glanced up toward Bridge House. There was no one milling about; they'd all crossed South Bridge by now to get to their cars. Or flew away or whatever it was they did. The only cars in the parking lot were mine. Well, my Jeep and soon-to-be Dimitri's red Corvette.

It must have felt like being in the water when she drove it. It had always made me feel free.

Before I could talk myself out of it, I slid my shorts and underwear down my legs, hiding the underwear inside. I wondered if my mother had worn underwear with her dresses and immediately banished the thought. I pulled my sports tank over my head, folded them all together, and put them on the rock nearby to keep the sand off of them.

"Here goes nothing."

I strode into the water far more confidently than I felt. It made me want to pee, but I remembered the warning about bladder infections with dirty water and held it in.

Norbert swam in a wide circle around me as I covered my breasts with my arms. "This is weird."

"I've seen bodies before, Misty. Do you know how many people used to come here and have sex?"

I shuddered. That was another visual I didn't need. "What do I do now?"

"I told you." He flicked his tail, splashing me in the face. Something like a chuckle emerged when I hauled a protest at him. "Just let go."

With another huge sigh, I sank further into the water. The smell of it filled my nostrils. Musty and stale, with an undertone of dead fish. "Why couldn't I find my tail at a beach in the Bahamas?"

I let the water reach my shoulders, and then let my arms float. Norbert swam back and forth. "Anything?"

"Nope." I shook my head. "This is not working."

"What happened when you found your tail last time?"

"I got drunk," I said. "Then I was too hungover to care, I guess."

"It was more than that," he replied. "You didn't just get drunk. What else did you do?"

I closed my eyes again and thought back. "I was happy, I guess. I'd apologized to Iris the night before and realized that I'd made mistakes, but that I had a chance to fix them. I was happy to have a friend again and thinking about the plan ahead." I opened my eyes to look at him. "I guess if I'm being honest, I was a little bit excited about fixing the house and having something to do all summer."

"You were happy."

I thought about that. "Yeah. I guess I was. At least partly."

"So, find your joy."

This seemed impossible. I wanted to transform so that I could feel joy. But to do that I had to ... find my joy? What the hell? "Shouldn't this just happen?"

"Sure, if you grew up doing it. But you didn't."

He was right about that. No matter how many memories came flooding back to me, I knew I wouldn't find one where I turned into a mermaid and swam. She'd kept it to herself. Maybe she didn't know I had it in me. Or maybe she'd wanted to keep it to herself.

The more I thought about that, the angrier I got. She'd treated me like an accident from the moment I was born and never gave me a chance to connect with her. Not a real one. And I'd been so desperate to please her that I'd done everything I could just to make her smile. I had been fighting a losing battle. And so had Pop.

I bet turning into a fish would have done the trick.

Right then and there, I decided to let that go. Iris was right. I'd do anything to make other people happy, and always at my own expense. So maybe it was time for me to figure a few things out about myself. Like whether or not I could become a damned mermaid.

The tingling grew, and it encompassed my body. To hell with it. I let it take over.

"Misty."

When I opened my eyes, I could see the sky. The sun had not yet reached its high point, which left it far enough behind me not to blind me, thank goodness. It was cloudless and clear and bluer than any water I could imagine. There was a gentle flap against the surface, and I lifted my head to see what it was.

My tail. I ran my hands along it, much as I'd done when I first discovered it. So smooth and rippled, with colors deeper than a picture. It gleamed in the sunlight, shiny and stunning. I let my arms reach overhead, pulling my ponytail out to let my hair float. A little bubble of laughter escaped me.

I turned my head to meet Norbert's eye and grinned. "Holy shit."

"Good job. Want to try and take it for a swim?"

I really, really did. I tested it out, bending where my knees would be to see how it reacted. It bent with me. It was heavier than my legs, but it didn't feel like I was *wearing* a tail. It felt like I had one, and I used that to slowly propel myself upright, swaying in the shallow water. I pulled my fingers in front of me. "Webbing."

"It'll make it easier to cut through when you go deeper. You gonna try it?"

The song returned, not the rough warp of hearing it through a shell. Crystal clear. "You bet!"

Before I had a chance to think too hard, I rotated and dove

head first into the water, flapping my tail until it pushed me forward. It was strange. The harder I flapped, the faster I moved through. At first, I let my arms drag behind me, frequently coming up for air and to see where Norbert was. "Why do you keep surfacing?"

I rolled my eyes. "To breathe obviously."

Norbert rolled his eyes right back at me. "You're a mermaid, Misty. You can breathe under water."

Woah. That hadn't occurred to me. I wasn't sure how deep Norbert could go, or if I swam too far away I could find my way home. But I pushed my tail and brought my arms forward, sliding through the water like a knife through soft butter. It felt like butter, too. Smooth and silky and decadent.

I spent the next hour or so weaving through waves, cutting in and out of the surface. I wanted to try one of those amazing flips in the air that I'd seen mermaids do in movies and TV shows, but I didn't think I had the ability for that. And I was getting tired.

Under the murky water, I opened my eyes and found Norbert. I opened my mouth to say I needed to go back, and found myself singing the song of my heart. I could breathe. I could sing. And I could see. A thousand little fish, a few crawfish who were too close to shore, moss floating through.

To my surprise, Norbert nodded at my song, as if he understood me, and together we drifted back to the sand along Bridge Island. We reached the shore, and I flipped onto my back, the sun now near-blinding, but I didn't care. I planted my hands behind my head and left my lower half in the water, flapping against the waves I had created. My hair barely covered my breasts, and the mental picture I had of myself was delightful.

I was a freaking mermaid.

When Norbert crawled alongside me I leaned over and wrapped one arm around him, squeezing.

"Thank you!" I kissed his strange snout, then spit out the salty taste of it.

"You just kissed an alligator."

"Well I have a tail now so I guess anything is possible."

I rolled back and closed my eyes, absorbing the sun. "I could stay like this forever."

"You could, you know." Norbert's voice grew serious, though it sounded far away as my soul hummed at the idea. "You could answer the call."

Why not? I'd already failed. I had no husband, no real home, and soon I would lose Bridge House. Aunt Ruth would be better off without me. At least before I got here there wasn't a bed in the cafe. And I wasn't helping people the way she'd meant for me too. I could barely transform myself without the aid of an alligator that I just kissed.

But I had ties to land. "I can't just leave Bridge House, not when it's relying on me." A dull throb in my heart cut through the song's call. "And my daughter Charley is on land. I could never leave her."

A shadow blocked the sunlight and I opened my eyes to see my daughter, standing behind me. Her mouth fell open, and she shrieked.

CHAPTER 9

"**M**om! Is that you?"
Her eyes were bugging out of her head, and she pulled her wild curls away from her face with wide-spread fingers. I scrambled to my knees, scraping them on the rock.

Knees. I had knees again, the tail was gone.

"Mom!" Her hands shifted to cover her eyes, and her voice raised in pitch. Right. I was naked. I stumbled to where I had left my clothes folded on the rocks and slid into them as quickly as possible. My skin was still wet, so they stuck to me, but at least I was covered.

"Charley! What are you doing here?"

Charley yanked her hair down. "What you mean, what am I doing here? Why are you making out with an alligator?"

Norbert had settled into his spot on the rocks to sun, reminding me just how fast he was. He winked at me. "I wasn't making out with him. I was swimming with him."

"Do you think that's better?" Charley's voice reached her shriekiest shriek, which meant she was about to scream. And Charley's scream could be heard for miles. Not that I blamed her. She'd just rolled up on her mother hanging out on the shore with a giant alligator. Naked. With a tail.

"Charley, I can explain all of this. I know it looks weird but—"

"*Looks* weird? It is weird!" She waved her hands at Norbert then pointed at my legs. "You had a tail when I walked up. A fishtail."

"Technically, it was a mermaid's tail. Although, now that you mention it, I don't know how they're different." My hair was dripping down my back and along the sides of my face, and a sudden wave of extreme thirst and fatigue covered me. "Honey, can we just go up to the house and have a drink? It will give you a chance to calm down, you can tell me what you're doing here, and I can explain all of ... this."

Her mouth worked, like she had something to say. She whirled around and stomped toward the house. I waved to Norbert and stumbled after her.

Her shriek returned when we reached the kitchen. "What the hell?"

Oh, yeah. Somehow, I'd managed to forget that there was a bed in the kitchen. I sighed. "It's been a long and interesting couple of weeks. Why don't we sit outside?"

I stopped her as she headed toward the cafe. "No, let's go out front. To the porch. I want to make sure I'm there when Aunt Ruth comes back."

I grabbed two glasses of Sam's peach iced tea from the refrigerator, making my way around the debris, and joined Charley outside on the porch. She was sitting on the edge of the step, just inside the last of the shade. With a surprised glance at my watch, I realized I was in the water far longer than I thought.

I plopped down next to her, my shorts making a squishing sound as they hit the wood, and handed her a glass. She clinked it to mine in a silent cheers. That had always been our thing, and it warmed my heart that no matter how upset she was, she was still my daughter.

"You look really different," I said to her. When she moved on campus to take her summer job before college, there were still traces of a high-schooler. But they were gone. "I love how wild you've let your hair become. And you look very muscular."

"I've been using the campus pool a lot. It's nice to have one readily available."

Almost against my will, my gaze travelled out toward the bayou. "Yes. A good swim is always nice." When I turned back to Charley, her brow was so furrowed it gave me a picture of how she'd look in twenty years with deep wrinkles and worry lines. I swung my arm around her. "So, you're doing well?"

Charley huffed out a laugh. She'd gone through a sassy teenager phase, like all kids do, but we'd always been close. Really close. And despite how calm she seemed, I wasn't sure how she was going to take the information that I was still adjusting to myself.

"Yeah, Mom. I'm doing well. How are *you*?"

I took a slow sip of my tea, hoping to soothe my suddenly dry throat.

"Well, you know. I recently discovered that I'm half-mermaid. Your grandmother, the one you've never met, was a mermaid. And the house is enchanted. Or haunted maybe? I'm not really sure about that part. But it's falling down and if I don't fix it we'll lose our family legacy." I shifted to one side to face her. "Also, Norbert is my familiar and I've reconciled with my childhood friend Iris who is a goddess and there are trolls on the island and a ghost who thinks he's Abraham Lincoln."

I downed the rest of my drink. Charley was staring at me like I had algae coming out of my ears. It was possible I did.

"Norbert is the alligator?"

"Yep. I'll … introduce you." Tears gathered at the edges of Charley's eyes, and she turned away from me. I wasn't sure what to say. This was much harder than the *where do babies come from* discussion. I wrapped her hand in mine. "Honey? Do you want to talk about this?"

Her shoulders shook a little, and she sniffled. "You just looked so happy out there. I don't think I've ever seen you look that free before."

A sick feeling settled in my stomach, turning the sweet peach sour. I had felt free out there. But I wasn't ready to admit that out loud. "I've always been that happy with you."

She smiled and shook her head. "I knew you would say something like that." With a deep inhale, she pulled her hair up, grabbing a rubber band from her wrist and looping it around until it sat in a massive pile on the top of her head. "It's so damn hot here."

"Wait, how did you get here? I don't see your car in the parking lot. You didn't take North Bridge, did you?"

"My friends like to visit Illusion Square in the summer. There are rumors that the air moves. I decided to tag along so I could check on you."

"What does that mean? The air moves?"

"I don't know, Mom. I guess that magic is real?" She grinned at me and nudged my shoulder with hers. I chuckled. "I met Iris by the way. She told me to tell you to come see her when you want to talk about what happened in the kitchen." She looked at me, gnawing on her lip. "Is she your girlfriend?"

"Would you be okay if she was?"

Charley's answer was immediate. "Of course. I really just wanted to see that you were happy."

I wrapped my arm around her, laughing when she shoved me off because I was wet. "She's not my girlfriend, she's just a friend. We're both into dudes."

"Are you into alligators? Because it seemed like you were making out with an alligator."

"Charley, I was absolutely not, under any circumstances, making out with Norbert."

"Is he my new daddy?"

I dropped my head back and laughed until my stomach hurt. Any tension between us evaporated. But a raw ache squeezed my heart. This felt free, too. Inside me, my siren sang in protest.

"What's with the bed in the kitchen?"

"It fell. Bridge House is pissed off I was trying to renovate upstairs." She dropped her head onto my shoulder, a movement she'd done countless times in the past, usually when we bickered or she needed us to feel close. I tapped my head to hers. "You seem to be taking this really well."

"Everyone has always said that Treater's Way is full of magic. I think I've always believed it. And I always thought it was strange that you never talked about Bridge House, or Aunt Ruth. Then suddenly you come for a visit and decide to stay?" She shifted to face me. "I know you need a purpose, Mom, but even for you that seemed extreme." She turned to look out at the water again, shielding her eyes as the sun was lowering directly into our faces. "It kind of makes sense. Is there more?"

I nodded. "There's more. But I'm soaking wet and starving, and there's a bed in the kitchen. Why don't we grab Iris and head to Treater's Way for dinner? We can grab Aunt Ruth on the way so you can finally meet her."

"I met her in the Square," she said rising. "She's a little goofy, but sweet." She extended an arm to help me up. "I really am glad to see that you are okay with the latest news."

"What news?"

Charley dropped her eyes down to her feet and rolled her lip between her teeth. "Oh, that makes sense."

"Charley, what news?" My throat was closing a little bit, as if the outside world was about to encroach upon my tiny little island. I hadn't realized it had become a sanctuary until now.

She squeezed my hands in hers and took a breath. "Mom, Dad got that woman pregnant."

CHAPTER 10

*G*ino's Pizzeria was the most popular restaurant in
Treater's Way, so it was only by a miracle that we were
able to grab a table on a Friday night. Charley and I
messaged Iris on our way across her bridge, managing to catch
Aunt Ruth on her stroll home. I was a bit worried she might be
overtired, but she seemed fine. Hell, she had more energy than me
at this point.

I couldn't wait to tell Ruth and Iris about my day, but my
excitement was tempered by the fact that my daughter had
stumbled upon me naked, a mermaid, and hugging an alligator.
She seemed to be taking it well, but I was a little on edge. Okay, I
was a lot on edge.

For someone who'd spent their life acutely aware of the world
around her, being freely naked was almost stranger than the
magical discoveries. And now that I was learning how to summon
my tail, and the call of the water was getting louder, I had
questions I hoped Ruth could answer for both me and my
daughter.

As we settled into our seats, Aunt Ruth sent a flirtatious wave
at four men in a nearby booth. I recognized them from my visit to
Illusion Square when we'd passed through to meet Lucas. They

were part of the Eight, whatever that meant. Ruth still hadn't told me.

"You have excellent taste in men, Ogo." I choked on my beer as Charley twirled her hair in one finger and eyed the table.

"They're all too old for you," I told her, coughing into my napkin. "And at least one of them is taken."

"They're all taken," Ruth tittered. "But that doesn't make it any less fun to bat my eyes." She giggled in her mischievous way and bumped Charley's shoulder. "I like that you called me Ogo."

I did, too. Old Great One, a term reserved for the matriarch, the leader, the revered head of a household or family. I wasn't sure it applied, but I sure liked how quickly Charley and Ruth had taken to one another. On the tails of that joy, though, was a fresh wave of regret. "I'm sorry you didn't meet Charley sooner."

Iris was perched at the edge of the bench, her long legs crossed and bare up to her skin-tight shorts. She had her eye on a man in the corner, half hidden by shadow, but she flicked her nails in my direction. "Stop with the regret already, it's getting tiresome."

Aunt Ruth squeezed my hand across the table. "It's as much that old bridge's fault as your Pop's, Misty. You're not to blame."

I squeezed back. "I'm not letting myself off that easy."

We placed orders for something called Sweep the Floor, which did not sound appetizing as a food product until you saw the ingredients. A little bit of everything sounded right up my alley. I sat for a moment, enjoying the crisp, tart beer while Charley, Ruth, and Iris got to know each other. Their chatter was idle and sweet, and I once again marveled at how well Charley was taking all these new discoveries.

I wasn't doing as well, but I faked it. The news about Daniel had shaken me. I was carrying the weight of an entire house on my shoulder. I had no idea which path to take.

But I wasn't about to let that ruin the camaraderie at the table.

When the food arrived, the waitress included a round of cocktails. "From the gentleman in the corner." She winked in

Iris's direction as she said it. I sniffed at the cocktail. It smelled fruity, with a hint of coconut. On a shrug I tipped it to Charley's glass and took a sip.

Charley grabbed hers hesitantly and eyed me. "I'm not old enough to drink this."

"You're in college, you live on your own, and you have a job." I nudged the drink toward her mouth. "Given the day we've had, one drink with your family won't hurt you."

Iris lifted her glass in the direction of the shadows, and the man leaned into the light to smile at her. Lucas. I groaned and put my cup down. "He probably put something in it so I'd be too sick to manage the house."

Iris drank without taking her eyes off him. "He wouldn't do that."

"Uh-huh. Don't you hate trolls?"

At that, she turned to me. "You know about him?"

"Dimitri told me. I don't get why you sneer at Dimitri but smile at Lucas. Especially when they are exact opposites on the inside. And I'm pretty sure he's behind all the mishaps with our renovations."

Iris rotated her body to the table, shock lifting her eyebrows. "You think he's capable of that?"

"It's a theory," I replied. "I can't prove anything. He gave me Buford's number, and while Buford seems nice enough I can't help but wonder about all the *little things* that keep setting us back." I dragged air quotes through the space between us. "He's at the cafe a lot more than he was before I agreed to his deal. And he didn't look at all sad when Mother's bed crashed through the house today."

Iris was thoughtful for a moment, sipping her cocktail until the ice shifted. Then, she took mine. "Lucas and I have a history. I'll agree that he's not always ... above board. But I don't think he'd go that far. Besides, he'd want the house to be successful. He needs it."

I paused with a bit of pizza midway to my mouth. "Why does

Lucas need the house? What would he do with it?" Iris looked across the table at Ruth, who suddenly found her plate very interesting. "Ruth"—I waited until she met my eyes—"what does Lucas need with the house?"

She fiddled with her napkin, and I bit my lip as frustration welled. "You haven't been completely honest with me, have you?"

Ruth sighed, a heavy sigh that suddenly had her looking every bit her age. "The house is special, Misty. And it needs you."

"Yeah, we've covered that." I wiped my fingers and pushed my plate away. Whatever I was about to hear was going to make me lose my appetite. Or, at the very least, twist my stomach into knots. "We have a connection, and I'm supposed to take care of it, whatever that means. But what does it *need* me for?"

"Don't be naive, Misty." Iris lifted her hands, as if somehow I was the one being dishonest. "Surely, you've felt it call to you, and you've seen that the supernatural gravitate toward it. I thought your memories came back?"

I stared at her. "I've already told you they have. But I don't have a clear picture of any of it because, even when I was young, no one told me the whole story. It's not all connecting up here." I waved my hand around my head. "So why don't you fill me in on what I'm missing, instead of berating me for things I've already apologized for?"

Iris blinked at me, and for an instant I felt bad and wanted to take the words back. But I would have been doing just what she always accused me of: sacrificing my own needs to make her feel better. I was frustrated and tired. I'd been fighting a losing battle from the start against people with ulterior motives, and no one had bothered to tell me why. They'd let me think it was just a house, and I was just a human. No one had bothered to correct me when I thought my mother left me.

I was sick of getting half the story. I was tired of feeling like everything was my fault. I snatched my drink back from Iris and tipped it back before slamming it on the table.

"So, what happens then, if I fix the house up, and we

somehow manage to get out from under Lucas's thumb? If I claim my family legacy instead of swimming away?"

Ruth's eyes held a sadness I'd never seen. "Bridge House is a way station for the supernatural, Misty. It's where they come to either develop their abilities or reject them. If they are ghosts, it's where they come to choose to stay and haunt or to crossover." She paused for a moment, letting me take in the words. "All of us who take care of the house are part-human. We're sort of like bridges ourselves. Our job is to guide them toward whichever path they want to walk, and help them walk it."

"And the house needs me because ...?"

"Because all the things I rib you about being are what make you the perfect mistress." Iris patted my hand.

I pulled away on a shudder. "I don't like that word."

"Governess?" Charley supplied.

"Am I ninety?!"

"Fine ... Queen." Iris rolled her eyes, but her gentle tone remained. "Your desire to help others, even at your own expense. The way you hyper focus on a project until it's done. The care you give and how you can *feel* other people's emotions. Like when you offered Dimitri the car on instinct or hired Sam on a whim all those years ago. You just know what people want."

"Makes sense," Charley said. "It's what makes you such a great mom."

Tears blurred my vision of her, so grown up and strong but still young. "Thanks, sweetie."

"The house chose you as a little girl," Ruth told me. "Even then, you were the one who knew what to do and how to make it happy. Which helped it supply everyone else with the power they needed to transition. But when Lara left, and Roy took you away, I stepped in because I had to." She smiled at me, her youthful smile. "I was never meant to run Bridge House. I did the best I could. But the truth is that it's yours, Misty. It's always been yours."

From across the room, Lucas tipped his drink at me, offering me that smug, polished smile that was slimier than the thick layer of grease on our pizza. The expression was so much like Daniel's that I swallowed bile. I didn't trust him, and in that moment, I knew why—and what—he needed with Bridge House.

Lucas needed the house for the same reasons my politician husband wanted things he didn't deserve.

Controlling Bridge House would give him power. And having a score of supernatural beings grateful to him for helping them cross their own bridges would help him not only keep it, but expand it.

Did he have his sights beyond Treater's Way? To New Orleans? To the state?

It struck me just how dangerous he was, in no small part because no one believed he was capable of much more than controlling a loan or padding pockets to keep the damn bridge from being built. But if he constantly undermined his brother until the bridge was his, he could be the one to fix it. And if he was whispering to the house about everything he could do until it believed he wanted the best for it ...

Well, that would explain why it had been fighting against me.

Earlier today, though, when the bed passed through. The house held the same pain I did. I felt it like it was my own.

Had he taken it too far? Misjudged the house?

One thing was certain. He'd underestimated me.

I waved my glass at him, smiling and mouthing my gratitude, even as I waged a silent war. Daniel may have used me to get to his position of power then discarded me, but I would be damned if Lucas did the same.

There was no way I would let him win.

Even from this distance, though, the call of the water was strong. To truly save Bridge House, I'd have to accept my position as its ... queen. I'd have to accept what I'd always known deep down. I wasn't leaving Bridge Island. The House, the people, and everything on it were my home.

But accepting that would mean ignoring the water's call forever.

I knew I was stronger than my mother. I didn't know if I was strong enough for that.

I listened to the happy chatter of my cherished daughter, my beloved aunt, and my new best friend.

Would these ties to land be enough to keep the song at bay?

Would my sense of responsibility keep me in the house instead of beyond the shores?

My shoulders tensed to my ears, and I closed my eyes to relax them. I couldn't abandon everyone I loved the way my mother had.

I had to hope I was enough.

CHAPTER 11

When I woke up the next morning, every muscle in my body ached. It was as if I'd run a marathon the day before. Which I suppose was partially true ... I'd swum one. Arm and back muscles I couldn't remember using were tight, and my neck throbbed. I rubbed at my dry, irritated eyes and sat up, wiggling my toes. Even that hurt. But at least it wasn't a tail.

The call had subsided somewhat, helped along by massive amounts of alcohol and pizza. Charley and I had stayed up late into the night catching up on her world and discussing the fact that she was going to be a sister. But I didn't have time to process that information myself. Not yet. For now, I had a bed in a kitchen I needed to handle.

And there was coffee to be made.

I trudged toward the kitchen, following the low murmur of voices to the crowded room. Sam, Kitty, Buford, Ruth, Charley, and Iris all stood around the massive bed. There were coils of rope sitting on the mattress, which I made a mental note to replace, and similar braids on each of the posts.

Sam and Buford stood on either side in the center, with Kitty, Ruth, Charley and Iris at each of the corners.

"Woah," I managed. "This is not happening."

"We got this, Misty. If we coordinate, we can thread the ropes underneath and then lift it up pulley-style." Sam rubbed his hands together and gripped the bottom. "On three," he told the room.

Kitty popped a bubble in my direction. "Coffee is made."

Bless her. I wanted it, badly, but I wasn't about to let Ruth pull or break something with this insane plan of theirs. I nudged her aside and took her place. Buford kept his eyes focused on the center, and, as Sam counted to three, we all lifted.

The bed barely nudged. It was heavy, sure, but something else was keeping it rooted to the floor. I sighed. "This is a wasted effort. The house doesn't want us to move it yet."

Buford looked at me, his eyes wide. "Uhm, ma'am, I know it's special and all, but a house can't want a thing."

"Uh-huh, and you're just a contractor." With that, I let go of the bed and beelined for the coffee. Filling my cup, I grabbed the nut milk Kitty kept on the counter for me, pouring it in and stirring. I turned around at the silence behind me. "What?"

Sam cleared his throat and glanced at Kitty. She rolled her eyes and crossed her arms. "He is just a contractor. A human one."

I paused, coffee burning my lower lip. Buford's face was a mix of confusion and awe. "Really?" I asked him. "But you're so big."

He chuckled then, a sweet sound that made me like him just a little bit more. "There's probably a giant or something in my family, but not for generations. As for this"—he patted his belly until it made an echoey drumming sound—"that's my wife's cooking. She likes me beefy, and I love her food."

"You grew up in Treater's Way?"

"Yes, ma'am," he nodded. "Born and raised."

"Do you remember me? From when I was a kid, I mean?"

At my question, his smile faded. "I do, Misty. I only have about 7 years on you, but everyone in town knew who you were. The future mistress of Bridge House." He reached up and removed the faded ball cap I'd never seen him without and placed it at his chest. "And I'm real sorry about this bed, and all the trouble we've caused. There were ... circumstances."

Circumstances. I knew what that meant, and I raised an eyebrow in Iris's direction to make sure she knew, too. The fact that she didn't meet my gaze told me she did. "Can I trust you and your crew, Buford?"

His eyes sheened, even as his nod was firm. "I aim to take pride in my work, Misty. Never sat right with me that something was coming behind us and fighting our efforts."

It was enough. It was all I had, really. I couldn't find another contractor, and maybe I was being foolish, but I wanted to believe him. "All is forgiven, Buford. We're going to have to start over, and we have a tight deadline. Do you think you and your men will be able to help?"

He fiddled with the plastic extender on the cap. "We'll do our best, but we're a month past now, and the work is going slow. Even if we pull it together, I'm not sure we have time."

"I think you're right, Buford. But we have to do our best. And the house and I need to get right." I let the coffee fortify me. I had a lot to think about, and decisions to make.

But not today.

"Buford, do you have a chainsaw?"

"Yes, ma'am."

"Okay, gang, here's the plan."

CHAPTER 12

J crawled into bed even more exhausted than I'd been
after a day with my tail. I had cuts and bruises all over
my body, my muscles ached, and my fingers were blistered, but the
cafe could re-open tomorrow and the house was on its way back.
While repairing the actual damage would take some time, at least
the hole was tarped over and the construction crew could get back
to work. They were shifting gears in the morning. Again.

"First things first, we'll tackle the porch." I whispered the
words into the air, feeling the house settle into contentment
around me. We were on the same page, the house and I. Finally.
"But we aren't done discussing that wallpaper."

With nothing to distract me, Charley's news about Daniel
and his girlfriend burrowed its way back out of my subconscious.
I couldn't imagine he wanted a baby, not at his age and with the
threat of a relapse always looming. This must have been her doing
or an accident. Either way, he would want to spin it for the press.
He'd just won reelection, but it was hard to get things done
without public favor. And he couldn't very well play the I-might-
be-dying card with a hot, young sidepiece and a new baby.

Plus, we were technically still married.

I hadn't harbored any hopes that we might reconcile, not really.

The pain of what he'd done was still too fresh for me to even consider forgiving him. I still remembered the moment I caught him. I'd gone for a swim at the country club pool, heartbroken after we'd seen Charley into her new apartment and she'd started her job. My nest was empty, so to speak, and with Daniel in remission and the election over, I'd had my future in question even then.

But Charley called just as I was about to swim, and I'd fumbled and dropped my phone in the water. So, instead of just swimming anyway and dealing with it later, I'd come home early and found them together. On my bed. My husband and the press secretary I'd been so friendly with during his campaign. I'd brought her cookies, and we'd discussed her jerk ex-boyfriend.

I guess she'd traded up. Or not, depending on how you looked at it.

He'd dumped me out of the house as unceremoniously as he could, and me forever the people pleaser, I'd let him. A raw flash of anger cut through the pain as I thought about it. As much as I'd done to take care of him while sick, to organize parties for fundraisers, and to generally be a great politician's wife and still a mother to Charley, he'd discarded me as if he were trading up, too.

Boy, was he mistaken. But he owed me. And he'd need me to make sure this didn't become a scandal.

Now that I was settling in at Bridge House, it occurred to me he'd done me a favor. I would have stayed moderately content and meek forever if he hadn't shocked me out of it. And forcing me to cross North Bridge may have been the nicest thing he ever did for me.

The sea called to me then. Or, the bay. I wondered if the sea would sound different when it called. Crisper, or stronger. I wondered if that was what ultimately took my mother away. What did the ocean sound like?

My heart stuttered a bit at the thought, and the call roared in my head. I had to admit, it was seductive as hell. Being in the water, in full mermaid, was the most free I'd ever felt in my entire life. After the first few minutes, it didn't matter that I was naked from the waist up or that someone might see me. I didn't care about pleasing anyone, and the pressure to take care of Bridge House, and the folks in it, all but disappeared.

But of course, I had my daughter. She may not be young, but she still needed me. And even if she didn't, I loved her fervently. Leaving her was not an option. I didn't care how loud the bay's call was, I couldn't imagine a world where I never saw Charley's smile again.

Suddenly, the walls started to bear down on me, and the air grew thick with pressure. I struggled to breathe, as if a weight were sitting on my chest. I tried to call out, but my throat felt constricted. I reached a hand toward the ceiling. Whether it was a lack of oxygen or blind panic, I thought my fingers might touch the ceiling it was so close. Then I noticed the webbing between my fingers, and the heaviness in my legs.

I'd turned mermaid, just thinking about the call. Gasping, I grabbed for the water on my nightstand. Rather than drinking it, I dumped it onto my face. Then I focused my thoughts back on land, shutting off the call until it faded.

Gradually, the weight lifted, and my breathing eased. I sat up in bed and wiped droplets from my skin, inspecting my hands and legs. I was me again.

The thought bothered me. What exactly did *me again* mean in a world where I was split in two? Being a mermaid was me. Being Queen of Bridge House was also me. Being a mother and a friend.

It was all me.

And that was what I'd have to figure out. How to be all of those things. Because like it or not, I knew I was going to be forced to make this choice eventually. If just acknowledging the call shifted me, what would happen if I fed it more often? If I swam with Norbert again?

What if I went out and never returned, just like my mother did?

I hopped out of bed and ran to the bathroom. The idea of it was both attractive and disgusting, and I retched into the toilet as if I'd swallowed saltwater. This was the choice I would be forced to make. But I couldn't make it until I understood both sides of the coin.

I knew the freedom and wild joy of being a mermaid now. I'd had a taste. But what if I embraced my role at Bridge House? What would that feel like? It would be difficult, but it brought its own joys. Or so I hoped.

I guess starting with that was as good a place as any.

CHAPTER 13

J kicked at the scruffy workbooks sticking out from my mother's Corvette, smiling as Dimitri jumped and let out a curse. He slid across the gravel to glare at me, his eyes zeroing in on the extended cup of coffee I offered. "I figured out you were coming before the shop opened to work on the car. I'm not much of a morning person, but if you are here you probably want coffee."

His gaze was as intense as always as he lay on the roller thing, contemplating. "You look different."

"I'm figuring some shit out."

He hoisted himself up, his fingers grazing mine as he took the cup from my hand. To my surprise, a series of shivers trailed up my arm. He brought the cup to his lips, never taking his eyes off me. "It looks good on you."

I swallowed as my mouth went dry. He was softening toward me, and it was more than a bit unnerving. Once I'd dug underneath his grumpy exterior, troll or not, there was a lot more to Dimitri. And he was hot.

But right now, I needed allies and information, not a romp in the sack. Besides, I'd cut my favorite bed into little pieces with a chainsaw yesterday, so it would be a good long while before I welcomed a man into it.

"So, the coffee is a peace offering, but there's a catch."

His body tensed up, pulling his chest muscles across his tight shirt. "It's just a question," I said, hoping to put him at ease. I didn't know which way this would go, but I had to take a chance.

"Okay," he said after a pause. "I'm listening."

"Whose side are you on?"

To my surprise, he didn't ask me to clarify. And to my even greater surprise, his answer was immediate. "I side with Bridge House. With Ruth, and you, should you embrace your calling."

I blew out a breath. "That came fast."

He flashed a smile. He didn't do it often, but when he did, I found it even harder to believe he was a troll. In fact, that might be the least believable part of everything I'd discovered. "I was only waiting for you to ask." The smile was gone as quickly as it came, and he scowled a bit as he cast his glance toward North Bridge. "But you have to understand, my allegiance to the House doesn't matter. Not really. I can't connect to it or help you with your purpose. My quarrel with Lucas is over that." He nodded toward the bridge, and the scowl deepened.

"You could help some, Dimitri. You could give me some information." I leaned against my Jeep, which had collected a fair amount of dust since I'd arrived and hadn't used it. I was surprised Dimitri hadn't dinged me for not washing it and decided to tackle that before he could. "And you're handy. I don't need troll magic. I don't even know what that means. I just need another willing body."

A flush heated my cheeks at the unfortunate turn of phrase, but if he noticed he didn't comment. His brow furrowed so deep it looked painful, and he sipped his coffee as he glared at the bridge. I waited. It seemed smart to keep quiet. "Huldrekall."

I lifted my eyebrows. "What-e-what?"

"Huldrekall." His golden eyes held me in place. "That's what

Lucas's father was, so I assume that's what his supernatural half is. It's the Norse variation of a troll, charming and handsome. They like to seduce." I snorted, and Dimitri laughed. "I imagine it's been very frustrating that his charms haven't worked on you. It's how he gets what he wants."

I finished my coffee and tapped the mug. "He's too much like Daniel for that to work."

"Daniel is your husband?"

"Soon to be ex. He hasn't reached out officially yet, but it's coming." The sun lifted behind Bridge House, casting first light on the rocky patch of the shore where Norbert liked to sunbathe. I watched as he slid out of the water and lumbered onto his favorite spot. "He's got a baby on the way." My voice trembled a little as I said it, and I shook my head to remove the pain of it. "But I'll deal with that later. What do I need to know about Hulkeball?"

"Huldrekall." Dimitri was watching me too intently. "He has a cow's tail, and he's very vain about it. And simultaneously terrified that humans will see it and know what he is. His back looks different, too. Kind of like ... a hollow tree."

"Gross." I shuddered. "So, he wants the house so he can control or gain favor with any supernatural beings that embrace their abilities here, thus giving him more power and leverage when he needs it, right?"

Dimitri rubbed his chin with the back of his thumb. "You know, I've wondered why he was so invested in it. I'd hoped it was a soft spot for Mom." He jammed his hands in his back pocket, as if he could keep from hitting something. "Your theory makes a hell of a lot of sense."

"And did he seduce Iris because she controls South Bridge?"

Dimitri jerked his head to me. "I don't want to talk about that."

That was interesting. "Why does she hate you so much?"

Dimitri's expression darkened. "That's her story."

"She told me she and Lucas had history. Maybe it wasn't romantic, but that was the vibe I got. You two never ...?"

Dimitri's head shake was fierce. And I believed him. Iris had something with both of the brothers, but I trusted she wanted what was best for Bridge House. I'd ask her about it. Eventually. "Okay, putting that aside, you and Lucas are fighting over North Bridge, right?"

"More or less." Dimitri began to pace, and I grabbed the coffee mug he'd set on the edge of the car to keep it from breaking. "I'm the elder. When Mom died, she begged me to take care of the bridge. I moved into the damn house underneath, set up the auto shop in Treater's Way, and did my best. Only ..."

He let his voice trail, and after a moment he stopped pacing but his eyes didn't meet mine. Instead, he dropped them to the ground. "Lucas is clever. And he'd paid off some officials at the New Orleans Transportation Department before I had a chance to assert my claim. I was slow about it, and mourning Mom. So, while I own the bridge in name, he has them in his pocket."

"Which is why you can't repair it?"

"Not that I know how to. I'm no damn engineer. I'm good with my hands." He held them up, as if I needed to see them. "I'm not very smart."

"Bull." I said the words softly, but they may as well have been shouted with the way he flinched from them. So, I put the coffee mugs on the ground and took his hands in mine. They were calloused, the skin hard. A worker's hands, much like my Pop's. I squeezed them and released them.

"That's the narrative the world has told you. Lucas more than anyone, I bet. Because it served him." I met his gaze, blurry as my own eyes filled. "Daniel used to do that to me. Subtle little ways he'd put me down or imply that I was only as good as he said I was."

To my dismay, one of the tears fell, rolling down my cheek. I let go of his hands to wipe it away. "I realize now, now that I'm here and the memories are returning, that my mother did much of the same. That manipulative way that people who are clever get what they want from people who aren't." I sniffed and blinked until my eyes dried. "But being clever isn't the same as being smart. And Lucas doesn't realize he's up against a politician's soon-to-be-ex-wife. I've learned a thing or two myself."

I squeezed one of his hands, then picked up the coffee mug. "Never let other people dictate who you are, Dimitri. I don't like my friends thinking they aren't worthy."

I could barely breathe under the weight of his stare. He ran his tongue over his lips. A song that was very much not a siren purred inside me. Then he took a step backwards, jamming his hands into his back pocket and plastering on his signature scowl. "Have you decided to stay?"

I thought about that. I wanted to answer the right way, but I couldn't lie to him. "I don't know, Dimitri. I keep thinking about my mother. About the choice she made. And you know, I may not agree with it, but at least she chose." I paused, listening to the siren in front of me, feeling the pull of the house behind me. "You know, I didn't know your mom. All this time and I'm just realizing that I barely knew mine, but I think she'd want you to either cross the bridge, or burn it. You know, metaphorically speaking.

"I figure there are a lot of others like us, right? Who need Bridge House to figure out what they want. And I'm tired of the Lucases and Daniels of the world taking that right from them. So, I'm going to do the best I can for now. I'm going to fix the damn porch and fight the damn bank and spend as much time with my tail as I can."

Something sparked behind his eyes, and it lit a fire inside me. He didn't realize it, not yet, but I could see the same resolve in him I was starting to feel in myself.

On impulse, I flung into his arms, squeezing his neck and kissing his cheek. Then I stepped back, laughing at his bewildered expression and outstretched hands. "I'm glad you're on my side, Dimitri. Just be careful." I patted his cheek and turned back to

Bridge House. "Lucas is going to be pissed when he finds out you're almost ready to claim North Bridge."

"I never said I was claiming the bridge." Dimitri's words were little more than a mumble in my ears as I walked away. I didn't argue with him. I had to trust he'd see it when the time was right.

In the meantime, the house and I had work to do.

CHAPTER 14

*N*ot even the rain had stopped us.

I had to admit, at times it seemed as if the sky was angry that we were doing something so mundane as rebuilding a porch. But, come hell or high water, we were doing it. Buford and his crew worked nonstop. I wasn't exactly skilled in construction, but I could hammer a nail and haul away debris with the best of them. Dimitri's troll strength made laying out planks and carrying materials much easier.

We'd just cracked midnight on the third day, and a brand-new wraparound porch, complete with a splinter-free set of stairs, was ready to be primed and painted. Just as soon as it stopped storming.

Buford and his men said their goodbyes with a promise to return the next day so we could continue the work inside. And for once, the pressure of becoming Bridge House Queen lightened from my chest. Progress had a way of making you feel like anything was possible.

I lifted my face to the sky, laughing at the fat drops that pelted my cheeks, twirling in a circle like I was a young girl again. Despite three days of very little sleep and way too much physical labor, I was filled with energy, and the house matched it. My very being vibrated with an excitement and promise that travelled the ground and engulfed Bridge House's foundation. We were on the same page.

"All it wanted was the porch fixed," I told Dimitri. He leaned against the door away from the storm, arms and legs crossed, shaking his head at me. But at least he wasn't scowling. Each time lightning lit the sky, his eyes sparked like a golden candle. I extended one hand. "Wanna dance?"

"Hell no." He flicked his fingers through his hair, sending a spray of water across the wall behind him. "I want to go to bed." Thunder crashed overhead as he said it, and the thunder echoed through me, halting my movements. Under the dull light of a work lamp, he blushed deep red. "I mean I'm tired."

"Of course." The sound that came out of me was not quite a giggle. It was more of a weird, choking guffaw. No one would ever accuse me of being smooth. "Thank you so much for your help."

The blush faded, lingering on his cheeks as they lifted with his grin. "This was a hell of a lot of fun."

On the next boom of thunder, the ground shook. Dimitri's eyes travelled the road to North Bridge, and the grin faded as if it had never existed. Something disturbed the trees, crushing the top of them. In a flash of light, a large branch's crack mimicked the lightning. It toppled to the ground, taking a small forest of smaller branches with it. Dimitri crossed the space between us and took my hand, dragging me up the stairs. "You should get inside."

Even over the gathering storm, I caught the worry in his voice. My heart thudded in my chest. "Sure. Thanks again for your help."

He was off the stairs and trotting down the road before I'd finished the sentence. Intense pressure swelled against my ears, and I stifled a yawn in response. Another tree branch snapped, disturbing a flock of birds, their black wings silhouettes against the cloudy sky as they fled.

Dimitri was right. There was an undercurrent to the storm, a sense of impending danger, and the wise move would be to get inside before whatever the hell was happening reached its peak. I laid my hand on the knob, but I couldn't quite bring myself to turn it.

The storm wasn't just dangerous, it was raw and wild.

It pelted the ground and created choppy waves in the water.

I needed to be out in it, even if I didn't understand why.

My siren song rose until it overwhelmed me, guiding me to the water, lulling me in. There was no ignoring this song. It wasn't singing to me.

It was me. I was the song, as sure as I was the house.

My wet clothes were shed, and I was knee-deep in the water before I'd realized I was down the levee. A bumpy presence lifted my palms as it stirred the water. Norbert, usually long gone by now, waited at my side. I grinned at him, sensing the danger and feeling the excitement all the way to the tips of my toes.

Until my toes disappeared and my tail emerged. I'd scarcely had to think about it. One moment, I was standing in the waves, the next I was below them.

The storm was a power of its own, and it charged the water. My breath was shallow as I swam deeper, letting instinct guide my direction. The lower I went, the less the tension of the atmosphere pressed down on me. There were no ominous strikes or musty odors down here. I didn't think for one moment about how I might breathe or what I looked like half-naked, my tail not having any light to catch yet somehow shimmering as it cut through the water like a knife in warm butter.

Norbert was behind me. Then beside me. I swiveled to face him and he gestured with his tail toward North Bridge.

Is that where you go when you're not on shore?

At his half-nod, I followed. What would happen when I reached the border of Treater's Way? Would I lose my magic and memory, gain legs as quickly as I'd lost them? Would crossing under the bridge have the same effect that driving over it had on me all those years ago?

I dismissed the tiny voice of worry with a flick of my tail.

Tonight, I was safe as a mermaid.

A large sandbar crossed the distance underneath North Bridge, forcing us closer to the surface. Norbert's tail created a trail of bubbles as it dipped and swayed. When I reached the top, I broke through and flicked my hair back, channeling my inner Ariel just for the hell of it.

Heavy pelts of rain smacked my cheeks. Lightning turned the ever-darkening sky bright. We were directly under the bridge, angling toward the island side of the shore. A small shack balanced on the uneven, rocky ground just past the piers. The house was tiny, with an attached garage and faded logs. Small hurricane lights created a path from the ground above.

Dimitri and Lucas faced one another at the edge of the lighting. Their voices boomed over the drumming thunder. Lucas's tail protruded from his pants, and it swished furiously as it slapped at the water. Dimitri hovered over him, hands flailing. I lingered in the water, unable to hear what they said, but fixed in place by their growing anger.

Their anger wasn't alone in growing. In a blink, they were twenty feet tall. Then fifty. Then a hundred before I had a chance to catch my breath. As they jabbed fingers and clenched fists, their heights lengthened beyond the shack, until I was angling up to see them, heads level with the treetops, bodies bronzed and massive.

Dimitri reached his height, but Lucas grew taller. His face was naked with rage, the mask of propriety he usually wore washed clean under the rain. I'd encountered them on the bridge when I first arrived, in human form and fighting not unlike now, but it had been Dimitri who seethed. Dimitri, who didn't bother to check his emotions. Dimitri who always wore a scowl.

This version of Lucas was terrifying. His hair flailed around his face like angry snakes. His teeth bared. He reared back to punch Dimitri, who lifted his fists to protect himself. Someone screamed, and it wasn't until Lucas's gaze shifted across the water, then down to where I hovered, that I realized it had been me.

He grinned pure malice, turning away from his brother,

leaning forward until his massive form filled my gaze. He showed no surprise at my tiny form or exposed chest. My heart thudded in my throat. My mouth dried. Dimitri latched onto his arm, but Lucas swatted him off as if he were little more than a fly.

The storm intensified. The water surrounding me warmed.

I couldn't out-swim him. If he wanted me dead, I'd no sooner dive into the water before he'd squash me like a bug. Lucas spoke, his voice louder than thunder, louder than the growing winds, louder than my siren song.

"Oh, good. It was past time you saw who you were truly dealing with, Misty. You were too obtuse for politics and subtle dissuasion." Lucas took another step. "Since you've turned my brother against me, we no longer have to play games."

Over the past month, Lucas had presented himself as little more than a minor annoyance, despite the full threat of him owning Bridge House. He'd snapped electrical wires and weakened floor boards and stolen construction equipment. He'd behaved like an impish child.

He stepped into the water, its full depth below his knees. With a flick of his finger he could send me flying. His eyes were molten gold lava. This was not a child's behavior. This was a dangerous troll who would do anything to keep the power he wanted.

My body tensed, my muscles and bones freezing as if made of marble. I wanted to swim away, wanted more than anything to escape the pure wrath he directed at me. But I'd only begun to discover my power. My communication with my inner mermaid was new.

I was way out of my league, and from the maniacal glee in his enraged eyes, he knew it.

But I wasn't alone.

A golden hand clamped onto Lucas's shoulder and whirled him around. Dimitri's massive fist swung, contacting Lucas's jaw in a deafening thud. Lucas stumbled backwards and I dove away, feeling the tremble as his foot landed in the soil below me.

Norbert circled me, screaming words I couldn't hear as blood roared in my head and panic drowned out any awareness of my surroundings.

Lucas rolled, gathering on all fours, flashing me back to the first night we'd met. Under the partially-hidden moon, I could make out the curve of his back, like the hollow of a tree, with speckled brown spots that stood in contrast to his flaxen skin. The long curve of the tail he'd kept hidden reminded me of an opossum, scaly and pinkish. I shuddered at the sight of it, flicking through the edge of the water, the tuft of fur at the end gilded and shaggy.

Dimitri yelled for me to go. Lucas panted in the water, catching his breath, the corner of his mouth swelling as I stared. Something brushed past me, nudging me as if to encourage my escape. That would have been wise. But I felt bound in place, my eyes following the wake of water swarming forward.

It was Norbert, swimming with a determination I'd never seen, agile and lightning-fast as he beelined for Lucas.

A fresh wave of dread made time stand still. The storm seemed to halt overhead.

Norbert's massive jaws lifted. I held my breath.

Snap.

Blood turned the dark water rust red. It filled my nostrils until I could taste its tang on my tongue. Lucas whirled toward Norbert, already swimming away, a Huldrekall tail trailing from his teeth. He dipped under the water, spiraling to avoid being targeted.

Lucas balled his massive hand into a fist, bearing his teeth, a wail of agony piercing the night.

I swam forward like a fool. I couldn't stop him from crushing Norbert, any more than I could keep myself safe. But I wasn't about to go down without a fight or let one of my best friends down.

Not anymore.

Dimitri had his arms around Lucas's neck, pulling him

backwards. I swam forward, using the distraction to reach Norbert. We surfaced on the other side of the bridge, doubling back towards the Bridge House shore, the sounds of Dimitri and Lucas wrestling like titans clashing.

Dimitri's yelp of pain halted me. I turned in time to see Lucas latch onto Dimitri, a large gash covering his right eye. As if we'd hit the eye of a hurricane, complete silence engulfed the night. With a move a wrestler would envy, Lucas lifted Dimitri into the air and tossed him straight down.

Dimitri twisted midair, his arms jerkily trying to control the fall.

But there was no stopping his collision.

A bomb exploding would have been quieter. The center of the bridge collapsed under the weight of his body. Shattered remnants of warped wood and rusted metal splashed into the water, rattling my teeth. And Dimitri broke the surface, creating a tidal wave that thrusted me up and out of the water.

My tail disappeared. Deep loss pierced my heart. And I was swept under.

Black teased the edges of my vision. My chest felt caught in a vise. Water forced itself down my throat and yanked out my breath. I sputtered and clawed at my neck as if I might loosen the noose around it, forgetting that I no longer had a tail until pressure formed behind my ears with a searing ache.

I kicked and flailed, panic wrapping itself around me until the water was colder than ice. Just as I became certain that I, much like the bridge, was about to meet my doom, the reassuring ridges of my favorite gator lifted me up and forward.

I hugged his stomach and squeezed my eyes shut until we broke the surface, the rain beating down on me. We were back on the shores near Bridge House, and the foundation of the house seemed to moan with the wind.

I threw up water and everything inside me, rain mingling with tears, every piece of me in acute misery.

A hand, rugged with callouses, rubbed at the small of my back in circular motions.

"I'm so sorry." Dimitri's voice held an agony that ripped my heart further open. "I'm so, so sorry."

He was back in human form, as was I, and I didn't think to care that neither of us was clothed. I pressed my head to his shoulder and wept.

"He won." My voice didn't sound like mine. I'd never heard that tone of defeat in myself before, not even when I'd been kicked out of my own home. "I didn't even get to finish the house, and he won."

Dimitri didn't respond, but he held me tight. Time passed, though I couldn't say how much. The storm evaporated, a strange humidity settling over us. I trembled as the air dried my skin and hair, as the adrenaline dissipated, as the harsh sense of mourning drained the last remnants of my energy.

"Misty." Iris's soothing voice pried my eyes open. Her hands were on mine as she guided me to stand, wrapping a towel I hadn't seen her bring around my shoulders. The windows of Bridge House lit, a beacon of pain that beckoned me forward. I attempted a step, wincing at the cuts along my arms and legs. Debris from North Bridge littered the shore.

"I've got her." Dimitri, a towel wrapped around his waist, parted the hair from my face. He swept me into his arms. "We'll fix this."

I didn't have the fight to argue. I didn't have anything. So, I dropped my head to his shoulder and let him carry me home.

CHAPTER 15

*S*unshine blazed through window shades I didn't
remember opening, warming my face and pulling me
from nightmares. I pried my eyes open and wiped crusty bits from
the corners, propping myself up to look around. I'd spent the
better part of a week in this spot, only getting out of bed when
forced. During that time, the house had remained eerily quiet. I
couldn't hear Sam and Kitty bicker from the kitchen. Ruth never
hummed as she passed my doorway.

Construction was put on hold. After all, most of the workers
came from New Orleans, and they didn't want to take the extra
forty-five minutes to drive to Illusion Square, park, and lug heavy
equipment across South Bridge.

With North Bridge destroyed, Bridge House had been
effectively cut off from the rest of the world.

Tears I couldn't seem to stop sprung forth again. I sniffed and
snorted, blowing my nose and adding another wadded tissue to
the growing pile on my nightstand. A stack of plates rested
underneath the pile, their presence sending a wave of gratitude
through me. I was supposed to take care of the house, to become
its queen or mistress or whatever. But I hadn't left the bed in a
week and someone out there was taking care of me.

I gazed out the window, shielding my eyes. The rains had finally stopped. And though I couldn't quite dig myself out of the heavy defeat I felt, I could at least step into the sun. I trudged down the hallway, bypassing the kitchen and any hopes of coffee, and swung open the front door. As I did, a song met my ears.

My siren song had been as silent as the house in the past week, as if losing my tail in the water had muted it. But this wasn't my song. This was a coffee shop ballad I couldn't quite place. I followed the soft strum of a guitar and the maudlin voice to the parking lot, where Dimitri's radio was perched in its usual spot. His worn boots jutted out from underneath my Jeep.

Rather than kick them, I plopped down in the gravel and rested my head against my mother's old convertible. "Why are you bothering? It's not like I'm driving it anywhere."

"True." The wheels of Dimitri's under-car roller thingy squeaked as he emerged. "Nonetheless, I made a promise, and I plan to keep it." His voice held the weight of the emotions he, too, must have been holding onto. I met his golden gaze, the intensity of his stare kept me from breathing. He wiped oil from his fingers and lifted his eyebrows until they disappeared under his thick, dark hair. "Do you plan to keep your promises, too, Misty?"

A sliver of guilt wriggled into my stomach. I'd wallowed for the past week, not bothering to check on all of the other people who must have been hurting. Living on the island was new to me, and I'd approached it so far as a responsibility. But what about the others, who'd grown up here or needed this safe haven?

Sam and Kitty would lose their connection to the cafe. Ruth would lose her home. Dimitri had lost his half-brother, and his last link to his mother. Where would Norbert go if the island was abandoned? Where would all of these supernatural beings I kept hearing about, already struggling to find us, go to figure themselves out? Would they be even more likely to fall prey to the Lucases of the world?

And why was all of that responsibility falling on me?

The burden of the last few months pressed itself on my chest, like a lead blanket I couldn't lift. The sun beat down on me, casting a glint on the bumper of my mother's convertible. In a flash, it was as if she were standing there, waving for me to hop in the back. She'd used the car as an escape, more times than I could count, more times than I could remember. We'd drive to the center of the bridge so she could dive into the waters below and find her freedom.

I'd had a taste of that freedom. But I'd also had a taste of what it meant to be anchored right here on Bridge Island.

And with the bridge destroyed, for the first time ever, I no longer felt pulled between both worlds.

I didn't like the idea of me and my mermaid being two separate entities, and one or the other of us being in control. That was the problem with the whole choice debate. I was, after all, the mermaid. And I was the human. And for the first time in my entire life, both the mermaid and the human, all of me, wanted the same thing.

A strange chuckle built in my chest and came out like a bubble bursting. "Wow."

"What?"

"Nothing. Well, not nothing." I shook my head to clear it. "Can you meet me on the porch in a bit?"

"Sure." Dimitri hauled himself up, then extended a hand to me. I took it, enjoying the thrill of being lifted to my feet by someone so strong. "The Jeep is done, anyway."

"Yay. I missed you, Bessie." I couldn't stop the smile his eye roll brought me. I patted her hood. "We'll drive again one day. I hope. On to the convertible?"

I hadn't realized Dimitri still held my hand until he squeezed it. "Only if you're sure."

There was a lot I wasn't sure about. A whole lot. How I was going to repair the house. If North Bridge could be rebuilt. What I was going to do about Lucas and my family legacy. And, though I didn't want to admit it, how to manage the developing feelings I had for the part-troll rubbing one calloused thumb against my soft skin.

But there was one thing I knew for certain. I lifted to my toes and kissed his cheek. "The convertible is yours, Dimitri. See you soon."

CHAPTER 16

*A*n hour later, I had assembled my new family on the porch. During the time I'd wallowed, someone had painted it a soft, welcoming white. The porch ceiling and the shutters along the front of the house were a friendly blue. No one claimed ownership of the work, but Buford had a suspiciously similar colored stain on his denim pants. Sam's eyes were a bit hollow, but he sat up straight while I paced in front of them. He held tight to one of Kitty's hands. She dropped her head to his shoulder, her third ponytail—now fully grown—resting on his neck.

Ruth hummed and kept her gaze toward the forest beyond South Bridge. I was curious if she had a true psychic connection to the Mighty Oak in Illusion Square, as she always seemed to be halfway with it, even when she was physically here. Beside her, Iris draped a flowing skirt over her legs and tapped one manicured nail on her knee.

We hadn't spoken since the night the bridge was destroyed. As I searched her face, red-rimmed eyes betrayed what even makeup couldn't hide: Lucas's actions that night had altered her view of him, and she wasn't doing well either. Once Dimitri reached us, I planted my hands together and rubbed them.

I only wished Norbert would come up this far, but this was a good start.

"First, I want to apologize to all of you. For someone always accused of putting other's needs before my own, I've been very selfish this past week. I didn't bother to check on any of you. In fact, since I've been here, I've been so worried about my path and my choices that I haven't been the person I used to be."

When none of them argued, I flipped my palms up. "It seems so easy for everyone. It seems like you've all just embraced the magic. Things that might be considered special or other anywhere else are normal here."

"Welcome back to Treater's Way," Iris said. "Did you finally figure that out?"

"Kind of. I mean, I've spent the past month or so trying to see the magic and understand it. Even to accept it. And what I saw last week ... I can't deny that." I wrapped my arms around myself to soothe the sudden chill over my skin. "But it's different with each of you. You embrace what makes you unique. And I think that's amazing. But I kind of thought it was just you. Just part of your personalities, I mean."

Iris shook her head. "It was growing up here, Misty. Even the full humans who live here, like him." She jabbed a finger at Buford. "Even they know there's something underneath what everyone sees. It's called Illusion Square for a reason."

A deep, sudden longing rose within. A new kind of call. "I want to be that comfortable."

"Why can't you be that comfortable?" I looked over at Dimitri, who'd stood separated from the crew on the porch until now. He sat a few steps from Ruth and dropped his hands between his knees. "What's keeping you from embracing all of this?"

There was something in the way he was asking the question that got to me. And as I thought of the pain in his eyes and the sorrow in his voice when he crashed through the bridge, I realized he was asking himself the same questions. He'd been straddling two worlds, too. And he carried as much blame for the state of the island as I did.

"Because I thought being that comfortable meant choosing a life at sea. I thought it meant answering the siren song, learning to use my tail, and becoming something very different from who I am now." I swallowed as my throat constricted, pushing down the threat of tears. "I don't want to abandon my family the way my mother did, and I haven't figured out how to be both Queen of Bridge House and a mermaid."

"Damnit, Misty." Iris sniffled, dabbing a handkerchief to the corners of her eyes as her lips trembled. "Don't make me ruin my mascara this early in the morning."

"Do you have a plan?" Sam wrapped one arm around Kitty, then reached his hand over to pat Ruth's shoulder. "No pressure, Misty, but we're all relying on you here."

"Nope." That same weird laughter bubbled up. I lifted my shoulders all the way to my ears, then let them drop. "But I may have the start of one. Something Lucas said the other night, about being done playing games, has stuck with me. He said I was too obtuse for politics. And it reminded me"—I turned to glare toward the broken treetops near North Bridge—"if there's one thing I know how to do, it's handle a politician."

No one spoke for a moment, and while my talk hadn't exactly been a rallying cry, I sensed the shift in their energy. That subtle undercurrent of hopelessness had been cut through, if for no other reason than we were together.

"What if we're too late?" Dimitri's voice was laced with worries that I held, too. Some part of me was terrified that, with the bridge destroyed, our tenuous connection to magic on the island was severed. After all, my siren song was completely dormant. And I hadn't felt the house since that night, either.

Even Walter was nowhere to be found.

But I was tired of living in the past. I was done standing in the middle.

And the only thing we could do was move forward.

I planted my hands on my hips and balled them into fists. "I guess we'll cross that bridge when we come to it."

MISTY'S LOST HER MAGIC, and she's running out of time to restore the island. Will her impending divorce force her to admit defeat, or is it the bolster she needs to embrace her legacy?

^^^Scan the code above or click here to read book three *Bridge Over Shifting Water.*

* * *

When a clumsy dragon turns out to be her scorching hot ex, will an independent therapist reignite an old spark or let it smother?

^^^ Scan the code above or click here to claim your copy of *Not Yet Old Flames* and join my newsletter.

ACKNOWLEDGMENTS

To my wonderful children, Charley and Gabe. Each day, you teach me how to be a better human and allow me to get lost in magic.

You are the reasons I stay grounded. I love you. Now get off your tablets and go swim!

ABOUT JB LASSALLE

JB (Jen) Lassalle is a writer of low-steam romantic and urban fantasy. She likes strong females, dimensional males, and found family friendships that triumph over nuanced bad guys you love to hate.

Jen is a New Orleans resident. The city, and the surrounding areas, serve as a rich backdrop for a world where magic exists and mystical creatures are not only real, but live among us.

When Jen isn't writing, she's hanging with her family and friends at a local park or coffee shop. She likes working out, which is kind of weird, loves yoga, and plays video games. Of course, she reads.

Jen and her husband have two kids. One is an avid competitive swimmer (which sucks up all their weekend time). The other is a daydreamer like Jen who plays the Mega Man theme on his guitar and kicks around a soccer ball.

Jen isn't great with social media, but you can connect with her below. Or, join her newsletter when you claim your copy of *Not Yet Old Flames,* a second-chance PWF romantic short.

facebook.com/jblassalle

instagram.com/jblassalle

Made in the USA
Las Vegas, NV
16 November 2024

11950654R00059